The Man Who Ate The World

By

RJ Ellory

Also by R.J. Ellory

Published by the Orion Publishing Group Ltd.

ABOUT THE AUTHOR

RJ Ellory is the author of fifteen novels published by Orion UK, and available in twenty-six additional languages. He has won the Quebec Booksellers' Prize, the Livre De Poche Award, the Strand Magazine Novel of The Year, the Mystery Booksellers of America Award, the Inaugural Nouvel Observateur Prize, the Quebec Laureat, the Prix Du Roman Noir, the Plume d'Or for Thriller Internationale 2016, the Theakston's Crime Novel of the Year, both the St. Maur and Villeneuve Readers' Prizes, the Balai d'Or 2016, and has twice won the Grand Prix des Lecteurs. He has received a further seven international award nominations include two Barrys, the 813 Trophy, and the Europeen Du Point.

Among other projects, Ellory is the guitarist and vocalist of The Whiskey Poets, and has recently completed the band's third album. His musical compositions for Universal Records have been featured in films and television programs in more than forty countries.

Ellory has two television series and a film adaptation in pre-production, and has recently premiered his first short film, 'The Road To Gehenna', (winner of Best Drama and Best Cinematography at the Canadian Cinematography Awards). He has also resumed work in the field of photography with his first gallery exhibition and a number of magazine features.

www.rjellory.com

www.whiskeypoets.net

www.lonelyeye.net

ACKNOWLEDGEMENT

To all those who have given selflessly in the pursuit
of peace, truth and the welfare of others.

1

There were times when Joseph's whole body filled up with a nameless emotion, as if the sun was in his head and the moon was in his heart.

Neither nostalgia, nor melancholy, nor some beautiful European sadness of another era, it was just itself. It was his own emotion, and no one else's.

His mind, crowded with words and phrases – poems, quotes, lines of dialogue from films and books – seemed incapable of absorbing anything more, and yet it kept on absorbing. His mind was a sponge without any apparent saturation point, like some bottomless pocket into which you could keep stuffing handfuls of cloud.

It had always been this way, or so it seemed. Ever since the moment he'd arrived.

Perhaps this was the nature of things.

Perhaps all of this was part of the process, the acquisition and absorption of information.

Until he knew what it was that he was destined to do.

Until he was needed.

At lunchtime it rained, but Joseph went outside anyway. The leaves of the trees grabbed at raindrops and drank them up before they found the earth.

He tried to walk between the raindrops, but they found him nevertheless.

His hair became damp and his skin became damp too.

He enjoyed the sensation, and he watched those who dashed through the rain with a sense of bemusement. He thought of Bukowski: 'People run from rain but sit in bathtubs of water.'

Joseph walked as far from his workplace as he could, while still allowing ample time to return. He did not care for the grief and small-minded complaints that accompanied a tardy return. Small minds needed small problems, and if none were available they busied themselves creating. Like ants carrying leaves along slender twigs. His life seemed to be crowded with small-minded people, and they carried their leaf-problems and forever wished to share.

At the corner near the library, a young man was seated on a plastic milk crate. Between his feet he held a drum of sorts, and he hammered out a hypnotic rhythm, and he too – just like Joseph – did not seem to concern himself with the rain. Perhaps people didn't hear him, the sound he made blurring seamlessly into the white noise radio interference of city life. Perhaps they heard him but did not dare look in case his eye caught theirs, thus instilling an obligation to put money in the coffee can by his foot.

Joseph did catch the young man's eye, however. He even smiled. He crossed the street in the rain and took a five-pound note from his pocket.

He stooped to put the note in the can, and the young man looked so surprised that Joseph laughed.

"Hey man, that is so generous. Man, you are a total dude."

"Yes," Joseph said. "I am a total dude."

Joseph walked some more, and even though he now had no money for lunch he did not care. Dudes, generally speaking, could skip lunch without a second thought.

"Seven minutes," Menella Smedley said.

"Seven minutes?" Joseph asked.

"How late you are."

"Is that so?"

"It is," she said. She wore an expression like creased tissue paper.

"Then I shall stay seven minutes extra," Joseph said.

"That's not the way it works, mister."

"It's not?"

"I don't much care for your attitude right now."

"Okay."

She scowled. The paper creased beyond recovery. "What does that mean?"

"What?"

"Saying 'Okay' like that."

"It means I heard what you said, Menella. You said you didn't much care for my attitude. I said okay."

She seemed momentarily flustered.

"Time is relative, Menella," Joseph said. "Time is both fragile and elastic. It is not clocks or sundials or calendars or stopwatches or anything else. Time is more like an emotion, more like a feeling, something intangible - - "

"What – "

Joseph smiled from the heart. It disarmed Menella and she dropped whatever leaf she had intended to give him.

"Did you ever have a day that seemed to vanish in a second...and you remember when you were a kid in summer holidays and one day lasted for a whole year, and you lay in bed at night and your skin prickled with sunburn, and you could feel sand between your toes and you didn't care…and even as you drifted off to sleep you could still smell the sea and hear the gulls, and it seemed like the whole of your life had been bringing you to this special perfect moment? Did you ever feel that, Menella?"

"I think you need some professional help."

"With what?"

"I think you might be a bit crazy."

Joseph smiled. "Probably, yes. You know, some people never go crazy. What truly horrible lives they must lead."

"That is totally mental."

"That, my dear sweet Menella, is Charles Bukowski."

She folded her arms. She looked like someone had crapped in her in-tray. "Well, maybe you and this Charles whoever should go and work somewhere else."

Joseph smiled. "Maybe we will."

At seven minutes after five, Joseph left his workstation. In his hand he clutched a small handwritten note. He placed it carefully in the centre of Menella's desk.

The note read:

Leaving work now. See you tomorrow. Unless something happens.

Lots of love, Joseph. 5.07 pm.

There was no reason at all to write *Lots of love*; he did it solely to let her know that he bore no grudge. The *Unless something happens* was just for himself.

Who said most of life's problems were solved with twenty seconds of courage?

Joseph believed it. He guessed most people could muster five, even ten, but twenty?

In twenty seconds he could tell Menella to go to Hell, chuck in his job, leave his flat, just take off into the wild blue yonder.

He could do those things. Not all of them in the same twenty, but one, perhaps two.

It would be a chain reaction, nevertheless. Take a step big enough to gain momentum, and let gravity and magnetism do the rest.

Joseph believed in gravity and magnetism. They seemed to him to be tremendously reliable concepts.

Soft-minded aphorisms and homilies did not harmonise with Joseph's perspective.

Words meant almost nothing, save where they were necessary to facilitate or encourage action.

There were real people who had lived real lives and said real things about being human.

These were the heroes: Those who accomplished things despite the discouraging words of others.

I went to the woods because I wished to live deliberately, to front only the essential facts of life, and see if I could not learn what it had to teach, and not, when I came to die, discover that I had not lived.

Thoreau. Mad bastard that he was.

The world breaks everyone, and afterward, some are strong at the broken places.

But man is not made for defeat. A man can be destroyed, but not defeated.

Hemingway. Drank himself to a self-inflicted shotgun death, but he lived a hundred lives and he tore holes in the world, and the things that fell through those holes could never be put back.

We shall tear a hole in the world, Joseph.

When he thought those words, it was as if he was listening to himself for the very first time.

Joseph stopped at the supermarket.

He gathered a few provisions with which to make a simple dinner. He bought a bottle of red wine. Spanish wine. He would drink the whole thing in one sitting. Tonight.

At the checkout a pretty girl with half a dozen rings in her ears and a staple punched through her lip smiled at him.

Joseph said, "Every man's life ends the same way. It is only the details of how he lived and how he died that distinguish one man from another."

"Does that go for us too?" the pretty girl asked.

"For us?"

"For girls?"

"Of course it goes for girls."

"Then why do you say *he* and *man*?"

"I didn't say it."

The girl frowned. "Sure you did. I just heard you say it."

Joseph laughed. "It was Hemingway."

"Ernest Hemingway said that?"

"You know Hemingway?"

"No, of course not. He's dead. He died a long time before I was born. If I knew Hemingway personally, I'd have to be at least sixty years old, more than that even." The girl stopped scanning groceries and looked at Joseph intently. "Do I look sixty to you?"

"No."

"Then you asked a stupid question, didn't you?"

"What's your name?" Joseph asked.

The girl glanced down at the badge on her tunic. The badge said *Melissa.*

"My name is Joseph," Joseph said.

"Eleven pounds, fifty-two, Joseph," Melissa replied.

In America they were called condos. In England, simply maisonettes, though that was a French word. Four flats in one block, each with their own front door. Joseph rented one such flat, and had done so for as long as he could remember.

In the flat to his left was Mrs. Young. She was anything but young, but she had once been young for a time. Like all people. Her husband had died in the Second World War and she had never married again. She was ninety-one, and her niece had recently moved in to care for her. Despite the niece being at least sixty, she played the coquettish amoreuse with Joseph. Her name was Margaret, but she told people to call her Maggie whether they wished to or not. She did not consult them on the matter. *Call me Maggie*, she said, like there would be a problem if anyone failed to comply.

"I am much younger than you," Joseph wanted to say when Maggie flirted with him. "You are old enough to be my mom. Don't do this. It's just plain weird."

But he did not. He didn't say a word. As the French liked to say, he kept his tongue in his pocket.

In the flat beneath Joseph was Frank. Frank was a window cleaner and a gambler. He took money for cleaning windows and bet that money on horses. He was laconic and reserved and his body language spoke of loneliness combined with a brave effort to conceal it.

"Compulsive and inveterate, that's what I am," Frank once said as if commenting on nothing more significant than a noticeable predominance of cloud. "A compulsive gambler, that's me. I went to a Gamblers Anonymous thing, but it was all a load of bollocks. Tell you how it works. It ain't complicated. When you're winning you think you'll win forever, so you go on gambling. When you're losing you think it can only be a matter of time before you start winning again, so you go on gambling. Then you go home without a penny in your pocket and you think next time it'll be better. That's all there is to it."

"It sounds simple," Joseph said.

"I said it wasn't complicated, and it ain't."

"Well, I guess that's that then."

"I guess it is."

"Aside from the rush."

"The what?"

"The rush," Joseph said. "The adrenalin. I get that when I'm bidding on ebay."

"You do?"

"Sure."

"What do you buy on ebay?"

"Books, clothes sometimes. Whatever. I buy quite a lot of CDs."

"You listen to a lot of music?"

"I do."

"I've never heard your music."

"I listen quietly."

"That's very considerate, Joseph."

"Thank you, Frank."

"You're welcome."

Frank's neighbours were Chinese. They kept themselves to themselves. The daughter was in her mid-twenties at a guess, and she was very pretty in the way that most Chinese girls are very pretty. Joseph had never spoken to her, and she never acknowledged his presence. He didn't think she was rude. He was just a *gweilo*. It meant ghost. Joseph liked that. He was more than happy to be a ghost.

Joseph did not eat TV dinners. He did not use a microwave. He did not believe that microwaves were part of some global conspiracy to under-nourish the population of Earth and thus make them more susceptible to subliminal messages in the ad breaks. He just didn't like the idea of molecular friction in his Stroganoff.

By necessity, he had learned to cook. He was as adept as he needed to be. He did not understand how food had become a religion, irritable chefs like misanthropic TV evangelists spouting expletives and demands for *firmer pastry*. It all seemed a lot of fuss about nothing. It was a spot of lunch, after all.

That evening he cooked chicken and leek in a cream and white wine sauce. A sommelier would have lost his mind to see it being enjoyed with a Rioja, but rules were as rules are: some to be obeyed, some to be ignored, some to be flagrantly broken.

For the fourth time, Joseph watched *Man on Fire*. John Creasy would drink what he liked when he liked. He drank a great deal of what he liked, in fact, and that led to a somewhat slipshod performance on the job. The girl got kidnapped, and Creasy had to get seriously mediaeval with quite a lot of Mexicans.

Joseph went to bed but he lay awake until just after one.

Then he heard the commotion. He got up, got dressed, and went to the front door.

A policeman asked him to step back inside, and Joseph lingered in the doorway of his flat and watched as two medics carried Mrs. Young out of the adjacent doorway and along the walkway to the stairs.

She was covered from head to foot in a dark blanket. There was no doubt she was dead.

Maggie followed on after her, glancing back at Joseph.

Her mascara was streaked and her face was anguished. For the first time she truly looked like herself. No façade, no pretence, no *amoreuse*. She looked like a middle-aged woman who'd suffered a terrible loss.

Joseph stayed until the ambulance went on its way with Mrs. Young and Maggie. No lights, no siren, the pace sedate.

Frank called up from below.

"She gone?"

Joseph walked to the edge of the landing and looked down at Frank's upturned face.

"Yes," he said.

"You know she was in the Special Operations Executive. Nineteen years old and she was dropped behind enemy lines into Nazi Germany."

"I didn't know that."

"All these oldsters, they all did crazy stuff during the war, Joseph. Some guy I met on a bus last week. Explosives expert, a commando…lived in the Malayan jungle on his own for two years. Malaria. They airdropped quinine and he just carried on. Blew up Jap train lines. Supply lines, you know? Scruffy old bastard he was with a mangy dog. You'd never think to look at him, but without people like him and Mrs. Young we'd all be speaking German and eating bratwurst and sauerkraut."

"You think?" Joseph asked, knowing that such a viewpoint was nothing less than racist stereotyping. He felt sure there were numerous Germans who cared neither for bratwurst nor sauerkraut.

"Makes you wonder, doesn't it?" Frank said.

"What does?"

"People dying…makes you think about your life. What you've done with it. What you're going to do. Like Eleanor Roosevelt."

"Eleanor Roosevelt?" Joseph asked.

"You're never too old to become what you might have been."

Joseph smiled. "I like that."

"Not a question of liking it, son, it's a question of whether or not you're gonna do anything about it. Don't know about you, but that crappy job of yours would drive me to drink."

Or to gambling, Joseph wanted to say. But he didn't. He knew that Frank was right. It was a crappy job. Dull and pointless. A monkey-with-a-tie kind of job.

He had taken it out of necessity. While he was waiting.

"So that's it, then," Frank said. "She's dead."

"She is."

"She'll see her old man again."

16

"Where?" Joseph asked.

"In heaven, I guess."

"You believe in that stuff, Frank?"

"You got to believe in something, right?"

Joseph paused. "Not necessarily, Frank. I don't think you have to believe in anything if you don't want to."

"You're a strange one, Joseph."

"So I've been told."

"How old are you?"

"I'm not sure."

"Not married, no kids, no girlfriend I've ever seen…I mean, what the hell, Joseph?"

"What the hell you, Frank."

Frank was silent for a moment. "Yeah," he said quietly. "You got a point there."

"Goodnight, Frank."

"Goodnight, Joseph."

Joseph waited until he heard Frank's door close shut, and then he went back inside.

He didn't sleep. He logged onto the internet and read as much as he could about the SOE until daylight broke through the curtains and announced the new day.

2.

"You're early," Menella said. "And yes, I got your note, Mr. Funny Guy. Very amusing."

Joseph nodded. He didn't say anything.

"You look tired."

"I am."

"Didn't you sleep?"

"No."

"How come?"

Joseph frowned. "Does it matter?"

Menella put her face on again. "I am your Line Manager, Joseph Conrad, and if you show up for work and you are not sufficiently rested then it will undoubtedly affect your work performance, and that performance will then reflect on me."

"Someone died."

Menella's face unfolded. "Really? I am sorry. Someone close."

"Yes," Joseph said. "Very close."

"Oh Joseph, I am so sorry. Might I ask who it was?"

"My neighbour, Mrs. Young."

Menella took a pause. "And you and she were close?"

"Yeah, about twelve feet to the left most of the time, dependent upon which way I was facing."

"How can you joke at a time like this?"

"She was my neighbour, Menella, not yours."

"I think you should get to work," Menella said, and turned on her heel.

At lunchtime it was not raining and Joseph walked to the art gallery. He studied the pre-Raphaelites exhibit. It was on loan from some city he did not know and had never visited.

He crossed the street to a small family-owned bakery and asked for a sausage roll. The girl behind the counter looked a little like Vera Farmiga.

"You look like Vera Farmiga," Joseph said.

"Do I?' the girl asked. "Who is she, then?"

"An actress."

"Is she famous?"

"Not famous enough for you to have heard of her."

The girl smiled. "I will google her."

"I'm sure she will appreciate that."

"You think she likes to be googled?"

"Don't we all?"

The girl laughed. "You're a funny guy."

"Weird is what people usually say."

"You just say whatever shows up in your head, or what?"

"That's usually the sequence, yes."

"Isn't it exhausting?"

"What?"

"Trying to be clever and funny all the time."

Joseph frowned. "I'm not trying to be anything."

The girl smiled like she knew a secret and was all set to divulge it. "Everyone is trying to be something, mister."

"Joseph," Joseph said.

"One pound twenty, Joseph," the girl said, and somehow she didn't look much like Vera Farmiga any more.

"Human Resources," Menella said.

"Who are?" Joseph asked.

She rolled her eyes. "Downstairs. They want to see you. You know where Human Resources is, right?"

"Yes."

They were waiting for Joseph. Two of them. HR #1 was a woman in her mid-forties, HR #2 a younger man with plucked eyebrows and truly overpowering aftershave.

"Joseph Conrad," HR #2 said. "Like the author."

Joseph smiled. "Same name, same heart of darkness," he quipped, but it seemed that HR #2 knew the name but not the oeuvre.

"We are seeing a selection of employees," HR #1 said. Her mouth smiled. Her eyes did not.

"Alphabetically," HR #2 interjected.

"Yes, alphabetically."

"Your name is quite close to the start of the alphabet," HR #2 explained.

"You don't say?"

Neither one responded.

"The company has been through a difficult year," HR #1 continued, "and we find ourselves in a position where voluntary redundancies are being offered. We are talking to everyone, of course, but we are beginning with those who have been here the fewest number of years."

"I thought you were going by alphabet."

HR #1 looked at HR #2.

"We are…well, we're doing it by number of years, and then alphabetically."

"So you have seen everyone who has been here for less time than me?" Joseph asked.

Again, they looked sideways at one another.

"Er no, Mr. Conrad…because no one has been here less time than you."

Joseph smiled. "So you've seen all the As and Bs, and now you're seeing me."

Again the sideways glance. They were a double-act with a limited repertoire.

"I am the first, right?" Joseph said.

"Yes, Mr. Conrad, you are the first."

"So what's the deal here?"

"The deal?"

"Voluntary redundancy."

"Yes, of course. The redundancies. Well, what is being offered is a month's salary for every year of employment plus a five thousand pound lump sum incentive."

"Okay."

"So that would mean…eight thousand six hundred pounds. Tax free."

"Can I think about it?" Joseph asked, and looked towards the small window to his right. The window went to another corridor. There was no outside on the other side.

"Well, these are just preliminary discussions - - "

The second stretched forever in Joseph's mind. Time was indeed both fragile and elastic. The past was a shadow behind him, and the years ahead appeared as fresh driven snow without a footprint in sight.

He thought of Thoreau in the woods and Hemingway on the wild waves, of Chaplin fathering a child at seventy-three, of Eleanor Roosevelt and Babe Ruth and Arthur Miller and Marilyn Monroe…and he saw the Vietnam War in his mind, playing out like a slow-motion film, and Marlon Brando running his hand over his shaven head and saying, *The horror…the horror*…and Dennis Hopper…*The man's enlarged my mind. He's a poet warrior in the classic sense. Do you know that 'if' is the middle word in life? The man is clear in his mind, but his soul is mad*…and there was music, great music, from Huddie Ledbetter to Sati to The Gun Club to Luz Casal to Debussy.

It all crashed against him and he knew that here was a significant moment.

He knew that this was the point where the waiting ended.

"Okay," Joseph said matter-of-factly. "Where do I sign?"

3

Paris exploded in his face like a jack-in-the-box.

Joseph got off the plane and smiled like a fool. He wanted to see the Café de Flores where Hemingway and Sartre and Camus sat and drank coffee and anise and people-watched.

He wanted to stand on the precise spot where Robert Capa had snapped that iconic image.

The girl at the information desk at Roissy looked like a L'Oreal advertisement.

She must have known Joseph spoke next to no French. She also thought he looked a little like Christopher Walken. A young Walken, of course, but possessive of something quirky and idiosyncratic in his features. She liked Walken. He seemed crazy, but there was not so much wrong with being crazy.

"You need some assistance?" she asked, and her accent conjured images of Jeanne Moreau in *Jules et Jim*, Catherine Deneuve in *Belle de Jour*.

"You sound like a French actress," Joseph said.

The girl smiled, gave him *that* look. *You are retarded, or you are hitting on me*, the look said. In truth, Joseph was neither retarded nor hitting on her.

"I want to go to the Café de Flore," he said.

"Well, that's in the 6th," the L'Oreal girl replied in her French actress voice. "It's on the corner of Boulevard Saint-Germain and Rue Saint-Benoît."

"Why do you think that a French accent is so seductive and elegant?" Joseph asked her.

The girl laughed spontaneously. The façade vanished for just a second, and Joseph saw behind the mask. He felt she was lonely. He felt that life had hurt her and she did not trust people any more.

"It's going to be okay," Joseph said.

"Pardon?"

"It's going to be okay. You will trust people again and the world won't seem so cruel."

The girl looked at Joseph as if he had carefully placed a dead mouse in her elegant French hand.

"I think I shall take the bus," Joseph said. "Which is the right bus for the 6th?"

Two glasses of anise, and Joseph walked from the Café de Flore along the boulevard and stopped at the first hotel he saw. The room he chose was expensive, but it did not matter. He had close to nine thousand pounds redundancy money, savings of three thousand, and a credit card with a two thousand pound limit.

He would make a decision concerning his life when the money ran out.

From the balcony window of his room Paris sprawled out before him like a dream. He had seen photos and films and documentaries, but he had never *seen* Paris.

It was all he'd hoped for, and more besides.

He kicked off his shoes and lay on the bed. It was twice the width of his own bed. He made like a snow angel and started laughing.

Maybe the destination was actually the journey.

Maybe it was that simple.

The same evening he took his dinner at *La Rhumerie*. He ate *assiette créole* and *banane plantain frites*. He drank a Zombie which was made with crème de cassis, sirop de grenadine and jus d'orange. He did not much care for it, so he tried a Hemingway. The Hemingway was good. He ordered a second.

A jazz band played in the corner. A black girl sashayed and crooned and smiled like she kept stars in her mouth.

Joseph forgot about the L'Oreal girl from Roissy and fell in love a second time in the same day. He knew it was fickle, but he was drunk and he did not care.

When the music was finished he waved the girl over. She frowned and shook her head. She walked in the other direction and did not look back. Perhaps it was establishment policy for jazz singers not to fraternize with the clientele.

Out on the street Joseph realized how drunk he actually was.

An old man with one foot sat on the pavement. He seemed intent on making sure everyone could see that one foot was all he possessed.

The old man looked up at Joseph and held out his hand.

Joseph fished a twenty-euro note from his pocket and gave it to the man.

"It will not get you a new foot," Joseph said.

The old man seemed baffled and amazed.

"But then, I don't think you are saving up for a new foot, are you? I think you are going to buy some vino."

The old man started laughing. He grabbed Joseph's hand and shook it vigorously.

Joseph laughed with him for a little while and then he went on his way.

The following morning Joseph walked to the Cathedral of Saint Volodymyr the Great. He walked on to the Église Saint-Thomas-d'Aquin. Churches pulled at him like some kind of magnetic vortex, no matter the city. He did not believe in God. Not in the historically-accepted sense. Perhaps there was a godhead, and we were all once part of the same unified consciousness, and then something happened and we all separated out to the far-flung corners of this universe and every universe beyond, and ever since then we have been trying to return home. But then again, perhaps not.

Churches were outrageous physical statements of faith. Joseph believed it was better to have faith than not. He appreciated the fact that people had spent thousands of years fighting over who had the best God. He wondered what would happen if they suddenly discovered that there really was just one. Or maybe that there was no God at all.

Joseph looked at the vaulted ceiling.

"Hey!" he called out. "You up there?"

His own voice echoed back at him.

Perhaps that was the only proof needed that there was a little of God inside everyone.

Joseph tried *andouillette* for lunch. The first taste was not so bad. The second taste was like someone had taken a crap in his mouth.

"It is a special delicacy," the waiter told him.

"I don't believe you," Joseph said, and paid the bill.

Joseph happened upon a small, art deco cinema. He watched a film in French, start to finish. It was called *Mon roi*, and it starred Vincent Cassel and Emmanuelle Bercot. Joseph recognized Vincent Cassel from *Mesrine* and one of the *Ocean's* films. He liked Vincent Cassel. He did not understand the story much at all, except that there was a skiing accident and a love affair. Nevertheless, Joseph watched the faces and the words they spoke, and the musicality and power of the language pleased him enormously.

Afterwards he walked back to the hotel and he spent a little while talking to the night duty man. The man's name was Jean-Louis, and his English was excellent.

"Where are you from?" Jean-Louis asked.

"England."

Jean-Louis smiled. "It is a big place."

"France is much bigger," Joseph said. "France is about the same size as Texas."

"Is that true?"

"Yes, Jean-Louis. It's true."

"And why are you here in Paris, Monsieur Conrad?"

"Because I received some money unexpectedly, and I felt it was time to discover who I was and what I was supposed to be doing with my life."

Jean-Louis said nothing.

"You know Mark Twain?"

"The America writer, yes of course."

"He said that there were two important days in your life. The day you were born, and the day you found out why."

"I like that."

"Me too," Joseph said.

"So you will travel the world to find yourself."

"I don't know about the world," Joseph said. "But yes, I will travel until the money runs out and see who is left at the end."

"That is very brave, Monsieur Conrad."

"Thank you, Jean-Louis," Joseph replied, and then he said his goodnights and went to bed.

Jean-Louis watched him go, thinking that this strange and brave Englishman looked a little like that Shakespearean actor. His name? His name? Branagh. Yes, indeed. He looked a little like Kenneth Branagh.

4.

"Sometimes we take the wrong road to get to the right place," she said. "Take me, for example. I am twenty-nine years old. I went to school like everyone else, I studied, got some qualifications…and I had all these dreams to be a photographer, and look at me now?"

"What happened?" Joseph asked.

"Drugs," she said. "I smoked weed. I drank too much. I got mixed up with bad people…and now I sit in cafés in Paris and men buy me drinks and I have sex with them for money. I am a whore. A putain."

"Yes, you are," Joseph said.

"I didn't even tell you my real name," she said.

"You don't have to."

"I want to."

"Okay."

"My real name is Emily. Emily Brontë."

"That's a pretty name."

"I am from Dorset."

"I don't know Dorset."

"There's not much to know."

"And now you live in Paris."

"I do, yes."

"Just so you know," Joseph said, "I will pay for our drinks, but I do not want to have sex with you for money."

Emily laughed. "I like you, Joseph. You are pretty strange, but I like you."

"I like you too."

"You know who you remind me of?"

"Who?"

"The actor in that great Spike Lee film. Can't remember what it was called. The one about a guy who has to go to prison. Edward Norton. That's who you look like."

"I don't know Edward Norton," Joseph said.

"And you have the same name as the writer."

"I do."

"Were your parents fans of Conrad?"

"I have no idea."

"You didn't ask them?"

"Nope."

"How come?"

"They were dead, I think."

Emily looked surprised. "You think?"

"I don't know what happened."

"Who raised you?"

"Just people, different people." He did not tell her that he remembered nothing earlier than a few weeks before.

"What, like foster families?"

"I guess so," Joseph replied. "I don't really know."

Emily looked away, looked back at Joseph as if she didn't want him to know she was looking.

"Are you autistic?" she said.

Joseph smiled. "I don't think so."

"You're not normal."

Joseph took a deep breath. "Banality and conformity are the suburbs of Hell, Emily."

She sighed audibly, like her body was a balloon releasing.

"I just don't know what to do," she said.

"About what?"

"My life. The fact that my life is in the sodding toilet. I'm stuck in sodding Paris, no money, can't get home, going round in circles. I am disgusted with myself. I want to see my dad. My dad would know what to do, but I am so ashamed of myself. I know that if I got home I'd figure it out. He would help me figure it out, but I just can't face him. I need to start over, but this is a vicious circle and I never seem able to break it. I get some money, and then something happens. Rent, food, medical bills, all the usual stuff. I never seem to make enough money to just get on a plane and go home."

"Is your lack of money the only reason you don't go home?"

Emily looked away, thoughtful. When she turned back there was a profound vulnerability in her eyes. Joseph could see the child she'd once been; the child she still was.

"No," she said. "Of course not."

"Your father," Joseph said. "Your father will love you no matter what has happened. That's what fathers do."

"You think so?"

"I know so. Like Thomas Hardy when he wrote of Geoffrey and his daughter. His concerns for his daughter made his heart feel inconveniently large."

Emily smiled. She fingertipped away her tears. Somewhere deep within her she found a well of courage and drew from it.

"I should just go home. I could make enough money in a day or two and I could just go home."

Joseph smiled. "Why wait? Let's do it now."

"What?"

31

"Put you on a plane home."

Emily's eyes widened.

"You can speak French, yes?"

"Sure...enough, I guess. For what?"

"There," Joseph said, pointing across the street. "That's a travel agency, I think."

He got up from the chair and held out his hand. "Let's send you home."

Emily started laughing. "Are you crazy?"

"Who knows?"

Joseph put her in a taxi with a plane ticket. It was first class.

The taxi driver spoke English.

"Take her home to get her things, then take her to the airport," Joseph said. "Here's money for the fare."

Emily looked out of the opened window at Joseph.

"I don't know what to say," she said. Once again, her eyes were filled with tears and the mascara bruised her cheeks.

Joseph smiled. "Goodbye, Emily Brontë," he said, and walked away.

"Who was that?" the driver asked. "He looked familiar to me."

"I don't know," Emily replied, and the taxi pulled away from the curb.

At the airport Emily Brontë called her father.

"I'm coming home, dad," she said. "I'm flying into Heathrow."

Her dad started crying.

"Don't cry, daddy," she said.

"What time does your flight land?" he said. "I'll come and get you."

"I screwed up," she said. "I'm a mess."

"We all screw up," he said. "Nothing matters, sweetheart. I'm coming to get you."

Emily struggled to breathe. "I love you so much, daddy."

At Roissy, Emily got thirty minutes complimentary wi-fi.

She updated her Facebook status from *Single* to *Going Home*.

Then she posted a comment:

A man called Joseph Conrad just paid for a plane ticket to get me home from Paris. I don't know who he is, but I think he just saved my life.

She added a selfie. Her make-up was horrible, but she was smiling.

She got forty-eight *Likes* before she'd even boarded, all of them from strangers.

"You are leaving us, Monsieur Conrad?" Jean-Louis asked. He leaned forward across the reception desk. He had a good smile.

"Yes," Joseph said. "I thought I might take a train from Gare d'Austerlitz."

"And where are you going?"

"I don't know."

Jean-Louis laughed. "Any reason for choosing that station?"

"Because of the battle...and because I like the word."

"Okay, well if you're going from Austerlitz, might I recommend - - "

33

"No," Joseph said. "I will know when I get there."

Joseph used his debit card to pay, just as he had done in the travel agency.

He took a train to somewhere called Montluçon. The journey was three hours. The ticket was not expensive. The coffee he bought in the restaurant car was very small and very hot. It cost three euros. He sat quietly and watched the countryside unfold. He tried to say the names of stations as they passed – *Bourges*, *Vierzon*, such names as these - but he knew his pronunciation was incorrect. The language was elegant, he knew that much, and though he had not spoken with many French people those he'd met seemed very friendly and accommodating. The old man with one foot. Jean-Louis at the hotel. Emily didn't count because she was from Dorchester, but he liked her all the same.

Regardless, they were all being someone else. They wore masks, and beneath the masks were other masks, and they carried so many masks – each for a different situation, a different conversation – and it all seemed so exhausting. French people were the same as any people really, but that was no surprise.

Joseph dozed. The ticket collector woke him.

"Montluçon est suivant," he said.

Joseph frowned.

"Next station," the man said. And then he said something like *Cans*.

"Fifteen minutes," a woman told Joseph. "Montluçon in fifteen minutes."

"Thank you," Joseph said.

"You are American?"

"No, English."

"You look like a very famous French actor from the 1960s," she said. "Jean-Paul Belmondo." The woman smiled again. Her face was old, her skin like chamois leather. "I am from Montluçon," she said. "Do you know it?"

"No, this will be my first visit."

"It has a lot of history," she said, "but then you are English, and you have a lot of history as well, eh?"

"Yes," Joseph replied.

"You were here," she said. "The twelfth century, but we drove you away in the fifteenth. In the second war it was in the free zone, but the Germans took over the rubber factories. That was a bad time."

"Yes," Joseph said. "A bad time."

"And why are you coming to Montluçon, young man?"

"Because I like the name...because I felt like I should come."

"Perhaps that is the best reason," the woman said, and laughed. "You are just travelling?"

"I am looking for someone."

The woman winked.

Then she smiled again, as if she knew precisely for whom he was looking.

5

"Maybe there's some sort of competition to see who can be the worst person in the world," Joseph said. "Do people get to the end of their lives and regret all those missed opportunities to be cruel and mean?"

"I think you have a very simplistic view of people, Joseph."

"Do I?"

"C'est toujours un peu complique," Jacques said. "We should know. We are French."

Jacques was the old woman's son. The woman from the train. Her name was Françoise, and she had paused for just a moment on the station platform, and then she'd invited Joseph to her home for something to eat. Joseph saw no reason to decline such an invitation, and so he did not.

"I read something once," Joseph said to Jacques. "An English writer said that the French had twice as much time as everyone else. They have the time we all have, and then they have the time they make…and they make that time for life, for friends, for people…"

"For dinner," Jacques interjected.

Jacques was a car mechanic. His hands were blue-grey with deeply-ingrained grease and oil. His face was like a leather satchel left in the rain, but his eyes were deep and warm and human. He was lonely, too. He had once been married but his wife had run away with a postman called Charles-Antoine.

Françoise, Jacques and Joseph drank wine together, ate some cheese, some ham, some fresh bread. Françoise then said she was going to rest for a while. She kissed Joseph on both cheeks and said, 'Enchanté, jeune homme. Bonne chance et bon courage."

That had been an hour ago, and still Joseph and Jacques were talking.

The bottle of wine was close to empty, but Joseph did not doubt that Jacques would find another.

"This writer also said that the French see everything twice, first to see what it is, then to see what it *really* is, and then they ask why."

"I think your friend has a very pleasant way of saying something that probably isn't true."

Joseph smiled. "That sounds like just about everyone."

"You do not have a wife and family?"

"No, I don't."

"And your parents?"

Joseph shrugged. "I have no idea who they are or even if they are alive. I think maybe they died when I was very young. I do not remember."

"And you have no interest to make this discovery, to find out the truth of your heritage?"

"No."

"Why not?"

"Because I am not who I am because of someone else. I am who I am because of me."

"Are not all influenced by everyone we meet?"

"I should hope so," Joseph said, "or there would be no point to any of this."

"I think the world is crazy," Jacques said.

They were in the barn that adjoined the property. Jacques had been showing Joseph a vintage car he was restoring. It was a Bugatti Type 35C from 1926.

"I think the world is crazy too," Joseph said.

"You cannot trust people."

"I think you can."

"You are young, perhaps a little naïve."

"Someone once asked me what was the difference between a child and an adult. I said that a child trusts until they are given a reason not to trust. An adult does not trust until they are given a reason to trust. At what point does the child become an adult?"

"When they are first betrayed, perhaps," Jacques suggested.

"Perhaps."

Neither spoke for a moment.

"It is a very beautiful car," Joseph said.

"She is, oui."

"When it is finished what will you do with it?"

"I do not think I will ever finish it."

"The journey is the destination," Joseph said.

"Exactement."

Françoise asked if Joseph would like to stay for dinner.

"That is really kind of you, but no."

She reached up and touched her soft chamois leather hand to his cheek.

"I think there is a light inside you," she said, "and somehow the world has yet to extinguish it."

"I think there is a light in everyone," Joseph said, "and yet we choose to extinguish it ourselves."

Jacques recommended a boarding house in the town.

"The woman who runs it is called Juliette. She and I have a long and interesting history." He smiled and winked, and then he shook Joseph's hand and kissed both his cheeks and told him to take care of himself.

"The same to you, *mon ami*," Joseph said.

"Ah, you learn quickly!"

Juliette opened the door and looked Joseph up and down.

"Jacques sent me," Joseph said.

"Did he now?"

"Yes. He said that you and he had a long and interesting history and that this place was the best place to stay while I was here in Montluçon."

Juliette laughed. "Then next time I see Jacques, *il recevra une claque.*"

Joseph did not understand the words, but the meaning was all too clear.

Juliette showed Joseph to a room on the second floor. It was sparse and clean and elegant. A small dresser near the window was shrouded in a washed-out blue gingham cloth. A mirror and a washbowl stood atop. The bed was old and sumptuously deep.

It reminded Joseph of a photograph he had once seen. An old photograph. There was a host of memories in the room and they seemed to welcome him.

"This was my daughter's room," Juliette said, "but she is now at university in Paris."

"I was in Paris before I came here," Joseph said, "But I did not see her. I saw a prostitute called Emily and I sent her home to her father. And a man with one foot."

"You are English," Juliette said, thinking at the same time that this young man looked a little like Serge Gainsbourg. "I like your Monty Python. This humour with a flat face...I don't remember what you call it. Something to do with cooking."

"Deadpan."

"Yes! Dead *pan*. I like this kind of joking. Very funny."

"Will your daughter come back tonight?"

"Tonight? No, not tonight. Clemence comes back only in the vacances. She is studying to be a doctor."

"You must be very proud of her."

"I am," Juliette said. "But she has boy troubles, you know? Always boy troubles. She is too much like her mother, I think."

"She has long and interesting histories with boys."

Juliette smiled. "Not so long for Clemence. Interesting, but not so long."

"Can I get some dinner here?"

"Of course, yes. What would you like?"

"No *andouillette*, please."

The chicken tasted like fennel. There was cream sauce and dauphinoise potatoes. Juliette served Joseph at a large table in the kitchen. There were two other people there, an American girl called Charlotte who had blonde hair and a contagious smile, and a serious-looking Belgian lepidopterist.

The lepidopterist did not speak English, and so Joseph engaged Charlotte in conversation.

"Where am I from?" she echoed. "I am from Boston. That's in Massachusetts."

"A New Englander."

"You know Boston?"

"No."

"I have never been to England. I would like to go to London."

"London is not England, just as Paris is not France and Rome is not Italy. They are world cities, not national cities."

"I know, but you guys have such cool history and stuff."

"We do," Joseph said.

"We have landscape and scenery and mountains, but we don't have history."

"You will. In time."

Charlotte smiled. "Are all Brits like that?" she asked, thinking that Joseph looked an awful lot like Casey Affleck.

"Like what?"

"You just say stuff and it's funny and smart."

"Yes, we are all like that. It's because of Monty Python."

"I *love* Monty Python!"

"So does Juliette."

"Hey, maybe we could go take a walk around later. I could show you Montluçon."

"How long have you been here?"

"A week."

"Why?"

"I am doing French as a Major, and I just figured it would be good to come and deal with the language in its own habitat."

"Makes sense. But why here?"

"Because of Nancy Wake."

"The New Zealand resistance fighter."

Charlotte looked like she'd been slapped. "You know of her?"

"Yes."

"That is incredible. I don't think I've ever met anyone who knew who she was."

"She was the most decorated woman in the war," Joseph said. "The White Mouse. She was the Gestapo's most wanted woman and she had a bounty of five million francs on her head."

"Exactly right. I am amazed."

"So what is your connection to her?"

"Tenuous, to say the least. For a while she worked as a journalist in New York. My grandfather was a newspaperman and he knew her. He was always very proud to say he knew her. That's all. I just wanted to see where she fought the Germans."

"It's a good reason."

"And why are you here?" Charlotte asked.

"I am looking for someone."

"Who?"

Joseph smiled. "I'm not sure, but I will know when I find them."

It was very dark when Charlotte came to Joseph's room.

He was on the verge of sleep, but the sound of the door woke him.

He knew who it was.

She stepped close to the edge of the bed and whispered, "Can I come and sleep with you?"

Joseph pulled back the covers. "Yes," he said.

She was a beautiful girl, and she was a beautiful lover. Kissing her was like sipping wine so rare it could never be priced or purveyed or purchased. Her skin was soft and warm, and when he touched her she shivered as if all the electricity in the world was in his fingertips.

She held onto Joseph as if she had been floundering in deep and strange waters and his body was a lifeline to a rescue vessel.

"That was amazing," she whispered.

"For me too," he replied, his voice that of a ghost.

"I don't usually do anything like this...but...but I felt..."

"Ssshhh," Joseph whispered. "No need to say a thing."

She rolled over and they lay front-to-back, forks in a drawer, their bodies curled like violin scrolls.

Her hair smelled of jasmine, and Joseph slept with that scent all around and inside him, as if drowning in flowers.

When Charlotte awoke in Joseph's bed she was alone.

She laid there for a while and wondered what on earth had compelled her to sleep with a complete stranger.

But that was the point. He did not feel like a stranger at all. Ten minutes and she'd felt as if they'd known each other their entire lives.

And yet, despite this, it did not surprise her that he had left without waking her.

She slipped out from beneath the covers and walked to the window. She inched open the shutters. The day was bright and fresh.

There, on the dresser, was a note. The handwriting was elegant and cursive.

It read: *Until next time. x*

Later, after breakfast, she walked into town and found an internet connection.

She searched Facebook for Joseph Conrad. There was a page for the novelist and a page for a bar of that name in Lowestoft, England. The man she'd slept with was not there. She realized then that Joseph Conrad did not know her surname. Perhaps he would look for her anyway, or perhaps he would just know where to find her. It never occurred to her to think that he did not care, that what had happened had been unimportant. He was not *that* guy. Not at all.

Charlotte posted a message regardless, even though it made no sense to do so.

Message for Joseph Conrad, she wrote. *Let me know if you're ever going to swing by again. Would be good to catch up. x*

An hour later, sitting in her kitchen in Dorchester, Emily saw Charlotte's message. There was no reason for her to see it at all, save the fact that herself and Charlotte were both in the Tiny Ruins Facebook fan club, and they had connected as friends. Friends that had neither spoken nor met. Later it would seem to be nothing but an act of fate. She *liked* it. She hesitated, and then responded.

Are you in France? Maybe we met the same guy. Contact me.

But Charlotte had lost her wi-fi connection, and the message went unseen.

6.

Joseph took the train back to Paris. He wanted to see the Pyrenees along the border with Spain. He arrived in Toulouse, was all set to continue through the Haute Garonne to St.-Gaudens when a man robbed a woman's handbag in the station. She was hysterical, shouting at the top of her voice for 'Assistance...assistance!', but no one seemed interested.

Joseph was not about to go haring after the thief, but he was willing to help the woman. Helping her was why he missed his train.

After a while a policeman showed up. He did not speak English, but he assumed that Joseph was in some way connected to the robbery.

Joseph tried to explain what had happened, but the policeman became increasingly flustered. He called for another officer. The two of them spoke to one another very quickly, as if they were in a film running twice the normal speed. To Joseph it seemed that they were having two entirely different conversations. Then the second officer took Joseph by the elbow and led him to an office at the back of the station.

Joseph didn't say a thing. He felt that anything he said might only serve to make matters worse.

The second officer sat Joseph in a chair.

His face was like an angry fist. 'Attend,' he said, and then he left again.

After ten minutes or so an older man with a kinder face appeared. He entered the room with a smile and introduced himself as Inspector Proust. He started to explain in English that there had been a misunderstanding. The woman had told him what had happened. He said that Joseph was now free to go.

"I have missed my train," Joseph said.

"I am sorry, sir, but there is nothing I can do about that. You understand, of course, that my officers were simply doing their job."

"It is their job to arrest people who help the victims of a crime?"

The man laughed until he saw that Joseph was not laughing.

"Do you wish to make a formal complaint, sir?" His eyes narrowed like a lizard in the sun.

"No."

"Are you requesting we recompense you for the price of your ticket?"

"I have asked for nothing."

"Then what is it that you want, sir?" Inspector Proust asked, thinking at the same time that the young Englishman reminded him of the actor, Jean Gabin.

"I want to go to St.-Gaudens. I came to see the Pyrenees."

"You can continue to St.-Gaudens tomorrow," the man said.

"But I wanted to see the Pyrenees today."

The man glanced at his watch. "By the time you get to St.-Gaudens it will be dark."

"Do the Pyrenees go somewhere else after dark?"

The man smiled awkwardly. "No monsieur, the Pyrenees do not go anywhere after dark."

"Good. Then I want to go to St.-Gaudens."

"You want me to have a police officer to drive you to St.-Gaudens? Is that what you're saying?"

"That would be fine, yes."

"And if I do not get you to St.-Gaudens tonight you will make some sort of official complaint against us?"

"I did not say that."

46

"But this is what you meant, yes?"

Joseph smiled. "What I say and what I mean are always the same thing. People only lie because they're afraid of the consequences of telling the truth."

The man looked edgy. He frowned a little, and then he got up.

"Wait here," he said, and he left the room.

He returned after ten minutes. He did not sit down.

"I have a man here who will drive you to St.-Gaudens," he said. "Fortunately, it is near the end of his shift and he lives there."

"That will be fine," Joseph.

"You're very lucky. Legally we are under no obligation to do this - - "

"Luck is nothing more than believing you are lucky," Joseph replied. "Tennessee Williams said that."

The Inspector seemed uncertain about what to say, and so he said nothing. He indicated that Joseph should follow him.

Joseph rose and followed him.

"This is Brigadier Alphonse de Lamartine," Inspector Proust said.

"Alfie," the Brigadier said, and shook Joseph's hand.

"I appreciate this, Alfie," Joseph said.

"Let's go," Alfie said, and he left the station forecourt in the direction of the underground parking levels.

On the way Joseph stopped at a *Retrait* machine and withdrew as much cash as was permitted in a single transaction.

The journey was close to one hundred kilometres.

"My wife and I hope to move closer to Toulouse," Alfie said, "but it is always the money problems, no?"

"Money seems to be a problem for everyone these days."

"Same as past as same is now, same tomorrow. Always the same. We are – how you say? – like when you are in the sea and - - "

"Treading water," Joseph said.

"Yes, we are treading always in the water."

The car was small and Joseph's knees were against the dashboard. Every bump and pitch in the road caused a jolt through his legs.

"I am sorry about the car," Alfie said. "This belongs to the mother of my wife. Our car is being repaired." Alfie sighed. "More money I do not have."

"Most of the time you get what you think about," Joseph said

Alfie shook his head.

"If you think about money problems all the time you get money problems all the time."

"Ha! It was so simple, perhaps! I should just think for more money and I will have more money?"

"Maybe."

"That is crazy, Joseph."

"Why is it crazy, Alfie?"

"Because that is not the way life works."

"I don't think anyone really understands how life works, Alfie," Joseph said. "That's what makes it so magical."

Alfie's wife's name was Madeleine de La Fayette.

"We do not take the man's name in France," she explained.

"Okay," Joseph replied.

Alfie had invited Joseph to stay for dinner. Madeleine seemed more than happy to include Joseph in their evening meal arrangements. Perhaps she was a little lonely.

"Would you like some wine?" she asked.

"Yes, please."

They drank wine together.

Joseph could see that Madeleine was pregnant.

"Our first child," she said, and she smiled so beautifully.

Alfie smiled too, but there was worry in his eyes. The child would be expensive. That was where the worry came from.

"Sometimes a child brings all it needs," Joseph said.

"Ha! I said the same thing last week," Madeleine replied. "I said the same thing to him. The child will bring what it needs."

Alfie laughed. "You are as crazy as each other. How many times do I have to tell you, that is not the way the world works."

"No one knows how the world works," Joseph said, repeating himself.

"Pah!" Alfie said.

The food was excellent.

"The food is excellent," Joseph said.

"It is rabbit," Madeleine said.

"I never ate a rabbit before."

"First time for everything," she replied.

"I don't much care for it," Alfie said.

Joseph put down his cutlery. "How much money would make you smile, Alfie?"

"It's not about how much money," he said.

"You never shut up about money," Madeleine said. "For you, everything is about money…or football."

"Yes," Alfie said resignedly. "You're right."

"It will be fine," Joseph said.

"It is difficult," Madeleine said. "I have to admit that sometimes it is difficult for us."

"I know," Joseph said. "But it will get better soon."

"If only we could break out of the trap," Alfie said. "Just one extra month's wages, even half, a thousand euros maybe, and we could fix the car, have enough money to move closer to Toulouse. We would be near to Madeleine's mother. She would help with the baby."

"After a while I could go back to work," Madeleine said. "I would like to go back to work."

"Yes," Alfie said. "We just need to break this…this…"

"Vicious circle," Joseph said.

"Yes, that's it," Alfie replied. "A vicious circle."

"We can dream," Madeleine said.

"Sometimes that is the best way," Joseph said.

After dinner, Joseph asked to use the bathroom.

Then he thanked Alphonse de Lamartine and Madeleine de La Fayette for their hospitality and for giving him the opportunity to eat a rabbit.

"Where will you stay?" Madeleine asked.

"No matter," Joseph said. "But I need to leave now."

Slightly puzzled, neither Alfie nor Madeleine challenged Joseph's desire to leave. They waved him goodbye, the pair of them standing in the doorway. Alfie stood behind Madeleine with his arms around her.

They looked like a nice couple from a Ladybird fairytale book.

At three in the morning Alfie got up to use the bathroom.

He peed on his own foot when he saw the money on top of the medicine cabinet.

He woke Madeleine.

They counted the money together. One thousand eight hundred euros. Exactly a month's salary.

They looked at each other and Madeleine started to cry.

"You have to find him and give it back," she said.

"You know we can't," Alfie replied.

"I know we can't," she said, "but I didn't know what else to say."

"Tomorrow," he said. "I will not go to work. We will go to Toulouse and see your mother and start looking for a new place to live."

Madeleine tried to remember Joseph's face. She struggled. It seemed indistinct. All she could think was that he looked a little like Yves Montand.

Then she started crying again, but she was smiling too.

7

Once Joseph had decided to leave the money for Alfie and Madeleine, he could not stay. Had he stayed they would have refused to accept it. Sometimes people needed to be given no choice.

It was dark and cold and he walked towards the mountains. At some point he would stop and rest, but for now he was not tired.

For a while he stood beneath the overhang of an ancient tree. The mountains were silhouettes against a midnight-blue sky peppered with stars. He knew each by name and by age, and he knew how they had been created.

After a while he sat down, and he must have closed his eyes for just a moment.

When he opened them it was light, and a child stood nearby and eyed him with an inquisitive expression.

"What are you doing?" the child asked. There was not a hint of French in his accent.

"You are not French," Joseph said.

"No."

"I was sleeping."

"Outside?"

"Yes," Joseph said.

"Why? Do you not have anywhere to stay?"

"I didn't plan to sleep outside. It just happened."

"You must be freezing cold."

"I am, yes."

"What is your name?"

"Joseph Conrad. What is your name?"

"Mervyn. Mervyn Peake."

"That's an unusual name."

Mervyn smiled. "I have unusual parents. They are a bit mad."

"Everyone thinks their parents are a bit mad."

"Do they?"

"Do you know Mark Twain?"

"No. Is he a friend of yours?"

"Kind of, yes. He said a funny thing."

"What?"

"When I was a boy of fourteen, my father was so ignorant I could hardly stand to have the old man around. But when I got to be twenty-one, I was astonished at how much the old man had learned in seven years."

Mervyn laughed. "That's very funny."

"You understand it?"

"Of course I do. I don't have two neurons, you know?"

Joseph smiled. "How old are you?"

"Twelve. How old are you?"

"Older than stars and mountains," Joseph said. He started to get up.

For a moment Mervyn looked anxious. He took a step back.

"I am not going to do anything," Joseph said.

"I shouldn't really be talking to you. I mean, I don't know who you are...and you could be like a crazy person or something..."

"I am a stranger, that's all."

"Yes. And you have to be careful of strangers."

"Because of what you see on the television?"

"Yes."

"Because the television wants you to think that there are crazy and dangerous people everywhere."

"Well, there are."

"Did you ever meet anyone like that?"

Mervyn paused in thought. "No, I didn't."

"A man called Groucho Marx said that television was very educational. He said that every time someone switched on the television he would go into the other room and read a book."

Mervyn smiled. "I like to read."

"I like to read too."

"But that doesn't mean we're not strangers, you know?"

"There are no strangers here, only friends we've yet to meet."

Mervyn smiled again. "I like that."

"William Butler Yeats said that."

Mervyn frowned. "Are you just an encyclopaedia of stuff other people have said?"

"I guess I am," Joseph replied, "but if someone has already said it perfectly well, then there's no need to say it differently."

"Makes sense."

"Yes, it does."

"So, how come you have nowhere to stay and you are sleeping under a tree?" Mervyn asked.

"Because I am a gypsy and a wanderer and I have no home."

"Why?"

"Because I decided not to have a home any more."

"That does sound a bit crazy."

"Maybe it does, but by whose standards?"

"Everyone else's, I guess."

Joseph brushed down his trousers and buttoned his coat.

"Did you have breakfast?" Mervyn asked.

"No, I didn't."

"Maybe you could come and have breakfast with us. My mom and dad and my sister are down there. We're on holiday. They rented a house."

"That would be nice."

Mervyn's father was a head taller than Joseph. He made Joseph feel uncomfortable on purpose, as if he had to prove to himself that he was afraid of nothing and no one.

Joseph knew that everyone was afraid of something or somebody, usually because they didn't understand it. Most times all it took was an honest conversation and everything worked out fine. Sometimes people told lies so as not to hurt each other's feelings, but in the end the truth always came out and then it felt worse. Better just to say it and be done with it.

"Who are you?" the father asked.

"I am Joseph Conrad."

The father smirked. "Sure, and I am Charles Dickens."

Joseph extended his hand. He wondered for a moment why he did not have the same name as his son. "Pleased to meet you, Mr. Dickens."

The father ignored Joseph's gesture.

"What are you doing with my son?"

"He invited me for breakfast."

The father raised his eyebrows. He turned on Mervyn. "What the hell are you doing inviting strangers to have breakfast?"

Mervyn smiled. "There are no strangers here, only friends we've yet to meet."

"Get inside," the father said.

Mervyn looked baffled. "Did I do something wrong?"

"Get inside, Mervyn."

Mervyn shook his head. "I guess you're not coming to breakfast, Joseph."

"It's okay," Joseph said. "I wasn't really so hungry."

The father squared up again. He seemed very agitated. Joseph sensed that there was something troubling him.

"I think you should leave," the father said.

"Okay."

"We don't want your sort around our son."

Joseph smiled. "What sort am I?"

"A troublemaker. Someone who talks to kids."

"Oh," Joseph said. He smiled again, and then he started to walk away.

"If I see you again I'll inform the authorities."

Joseph paused for a moment. He looked closely at the man. "Does it hurt?"

"What are you talking about? Does what hurt?"

"Being so angry and suspicious all the time. Feeling like everyone is trying to steal something from you."

The man looked more angry, if such a thing was possible. "Get the hell out of here," he said. Then he added, "Seriously, you need to get the hell out of here."

Joseph smiled. "Please tell your son it was a pleasure to meet him."

The man advanced a step, his shoulders tense. To him, this troublemaker looked tough. He looked like a young Ray Winstone, but if it came to it he believed he could beat him up.

Joseph smiled, and then he walked away.

Joseph reached the pathway down from the trees. At the same time, Alphonse de Lamartine and Madeleine de La Fayette, penned a message on their Facebook page.

Last night a stranger called Joseph Conrad came to our house. He ate dinner with us. After he left we found a lot of money in the bathroom. He put it there for us. He wanted to help us. We don't know anything about him, but we just want to say thank you from the bottom of our hearts.

Those were the words, but they wrote them in French.

Within two hours it had been shared by forty-eight people and more than seven hundred people had liked it.

Emily saw it, as did Charlotte. Both of them felt a strange sense of spiritual connection to the couple in France, and this they could not explain.

8

After four days, Joseph felt he'd seen enough of France to understand it. The words were all different, but the emotions behind them were the same. People were afraid, angry, anxious, reconciled and resigned; they were complacent, industrious, aggressive and reticent. They were kind, compassionate, thoughtful and empathetic; they were all the things it was possible to be, and yet they all wanted the same thing. Enough to eat, a safe place to sleep, a reason to get up in the morning. Most of all they wanted to love someone and to be loved an equal measure in return.

At Roissy, Joseph scanned the departures board. He felt a pull to Istanbul, but he chose Dublin instead. He bought a Business Class ticket, and he was asked if he collected air miles.

"No," he said, "but if you want me to collect them I will. Where are they?"

The lady at the desk smiled.

"You can just log onto our website, create an account, use the reference number on your ticket and they will be registered."

"Thank you," Joseph said.

"You're very welcome, sir," the lady said, and she smiled like she meant it.

On the plane he was offered a sandwich and a drink.

He accepted both. The sandwich was dry and tasteless, the drink too hot to finish before they came back to take his cup.

Joseph took the magazine from the pocket ahead of him. He read an article about Machu Picchu, and then an interview with Matthew

McConaughey.   Machu Picchu sounded fascinating, and Matthew McConaughey felt that taking yourself seriously was a big mistake. Joseph could agree with that sentiment. He felt that he and Mr. McConaughey would get along just fine.

When the flight landed he was allowed off the plane before everyone else. He did not have any luggage. He had been wearing the same things since he'd left. It was good that he was not prone to body odour.

He took a taxi to the centre of the city, and there he found a department store called Arnotts.

He bought everything – trousers, shirt, an overcoat, underwear, socks, a stout pair of shoes, and then he paid for it all and asked to use the changing room.   The assistant seemed all too eager to help.   Joseph changed into his new clothes, put everything he had been wearing into one of the bags, and then put that bag into a waste bin in the street outside. He felt smart and fresh and ready for action.

He found a place called The Winding Stair that was both a bookshop and a restaurant.

In the back there were second-hand books. Second-hand books were special. Sometimes you could feel how many times they had been read, how many people had loved them. Sometimes there were messages and dates, dedications and epithets.

A man with a blue sweater asked Joseph if he needed any help.

"No, thank you," Joseph said, and smiled.

"Just browsing," the man said. "Take your time.   If there's anything you need, let me know."

"I will," Joseph said. "That's very kind."

Joseph selected a battered copy of *The Wild Palms* by William Faulkner. He used the Page 68 method. Look at Page 68. If something makes you smile or intrigues you, buy the book. In this case it was the phrase, *In the drizzling darkness again he said to the plump convict: 'Well your partner beat you. He's free. He's done served his time out but you've got a right far piece to go yet.' 'Yah,' the plump convict said. 'Free. He can have it.'*

First the drizzling darkness, then the plump convict. Joseph bought the book because of the plump convict who didn't care to be free.

Upstairs, in the restaurant, a girl called Selina found him a table and a menu. He ordered McLoughlin's smoked bacon chop, crushed turnip and black pudding hash, Savoy cabbage and Dalkey mustard gravy.

"Would you like a glass of wine?" Selina asked.

"I like red wine," Joseph said.

"Me too," she said.

"Make a recommendation," Joseph said.

"We have an Australian Syrah called Innocent Bystander - - "

"Yes," Joseph said. "Please. That is a good name for a wine."

Selina was momentarily awkward, and then she wrote down the order. She started to walk away.

"I am Joseph," he said. "I will sit here and read my book."

"Er…good," she said. "I hope it's a good book."

"They all are," he said. "Every book ever written is the best book ever written for someone."

"I never thought about it like that," she said.

"That's why we all have to keep talking to each other. So that we have a chance to see things through someone else's eyes."

Selina smiled. "I'll get your order to the kitchen," she said, thinking that he really was very handsome. He looked like Matt Damon, but untidy around the edges.

Joseph opened the musty dog-eared book, and he went down the stairs with the doctor to see who was knocking the door so late at night. The flashlight lanced on ahead of them into the darkness.

Joseph walked after he had eaten. He had taken a second glass of Innocent Bystander and felt lightheaded. Faulkner seemed slightly mad, but he spun a tremendous yarn.

The river was beautiful in the late afternoon light. Children played. Dogs eyed one another suspiciously and then tried to make friends despite their owners.

A middle-aged woman stood on the pavement, an expression on her face as if she had never understood anything, perhaps never would. It was a reverie. When Joseph neared her he smiled and said, "I guess it all comes out right in the end," and the woman laughed and said, "Is that the way of it now, is it?"

"Yes," Joseph replied. "That's the way it is. Newspapers, television, all lies. It's not so bad as they tell us, and we all have ways to make it better."

"I'd agree wit' that, so I would," the woman said.

"I need somewhere to stay," Joseph said. "Do you have any recommendations?"

"Money is an issue?"

"No," Joseph said, and smiled.

"Oh, aren't we the grand gentleman today," she replied. "Well, if money'll not be a problem, I'd be gettin' myself into the Fitzwilliam or the Shelbourne?"

"Are they old?"

"Oh it's old you'd be after, I'd guess the Merrion is your safest bet if you're walkin'.

The woman pointed the way to St. Stephen's Green. "Ten, fifteen minute walk depending if you're keen."

"No hurry. Time is not against me today."

The woman looked at him with crooked eyes. "Ye are an odd one, mister."

"Conrad," he said. "Joseph Conrad."

"Like the novelist."

"Just the same. And what is your name?"

"Dorothea," she said. "Dorothea Du Bois."

"A fine name," Joseph said.

"Thank you, Mr. Conrad."

The Merrion was four townhouses stitched together by time. Inside it smelled of leather and linen, fresh coffee, beeswax polish and carpets that had seen the tread of feet for a hundred years or more. The girl at the desk smiled like summer.

"I would like a room," Joseph said.

"A room or a suite, sir?"

"I'd like a suite."

"Might I recommend the Merrion Suite, sir." Her name was Anna and she smiled again like the sun had taken up residence in her throat. "It boasts a king-size bed, a dining room to seat four, a sitting area, armchairs, a fireplace…all of it decorated in keeping with the original eighteenth century architecture. The Merrion Suites are in the Georgian Main House overlooking the garden."

"Yes," Joseph said.

"And it has free wi-fi, multi-line telephones, video conferencing - - "

"I won't be requiring any of those," Joseph said.

"And will sir be staying alone?"

"Yes, he will."

"And how long is sir planning on being with us?"

Joseph smiled at Anna. "Sir does not know."

Anna smiled back. It had become a contest, it seemed. "If you could perhaps give me an idea, then I may be able to apply a discounted rate for additional days."

"Money is no object," Joseph said. "I will pay whatever it costs. I like it here."

"Excellent," she said. "Might I take a card?"

Joseph gave her his bankcard. She swiped it, then asked if Joseph required a porter to carry his luggage.

"No luggage," Joseph said.

"Oh," Anna replied.

"Don't you think we all spend too much time carrying unnecessary luggage?" he said, but she sensed it was a rhetorical question and thus did not reply.

"I'll have a porter show you the way," she said, and returned the bankcard.

The room was perfect.

Joseph was there no more than ten minutes before there was a knock at the door.

Joseph opened it to find a young man in uniform standing there. He wore a bellhop's hat at a jaunty angle.

"James," he said. "James Joyce."

"Conrad," Joseph replied. "Joseph Conrad."

"I am the suite concierge," James said. "You pick up your phone and I am there."

"Like a genie."

"Just like a genie."

"Anything you'll be wantin', I'm your man."

"Excellent. I should like some tea."

"And what kind of tea would you care for today, sir?"

"Earl Grey."

"An excellent choice if I might be so bold. Anything else?"

"That will be fine, James."

"Do you mind me asking you a question, sir?"

"No, not at all."

"Did anyone ever tell you how much you look like Paul Newman?"

"No. No one ever said that to me, James."

"Well you do. You look a lot like Paul Newman."

Joseph closed the door. He crossed the room to the window and looked down into the gardens.

9

It was James Joyce who told him about the ghost.

"I believe in ghosts," Joseph said. "Always have."

"I don't know who it is," James said, "but I think it's a girl, and I think she died in that room down there." He indicated the far end of the hallway with a nod of his head. "People stay there…they say it's cold even in summer. I don't get scared in there. Not really. It's not that kind of thing - - "

"It's more a kind of sadness," Joseph said.

"Yes! Exactly! That's exactly what it is."

Joseph nodded sagely. "I have heard of this sort of thing before."

"Do you believe that people can haunt places after they're dead?"

Joseph smiled. "Yes, of course. We are all ghosts, aren't we? Some of us have bodies, and some don't. The soul is just a ghost."

"Do you believe in Heaven?"

"No."

"So you don't believe in Hell either?"

"The mind is a universe and can make a heaven of hell, a hell of heaven." Joseph paused, and then added, "John Milton."

"Do you think we make our own Heaven and Hell by the way we are towards ourselves and others?" James asked.

"I don't know," Joseph replied. "I am just a person like you."

"Room thirty-three," James said.

The girl's name was Violet Florence Martin and she died when a blood vessel burst in her brain. Violet was eleven and a half years old. A few weeks later Violet's older brother was shot through the face during the

Battle of Neuve Chapelle. These events were sudden and terrible and her family never recovered. Violet's father drank himself insensate, while Violet's mother watched with a hollowness in her heart that she knew would never mend.

It all happened in 1915.

How Joseph knew this, he did not know. Perhaps it was a premonition, a perception, a guess. He stood in the room in darkness while the hotel breathed with the sound of sleepers, and he allowed his mind to find the pictures and the feelings that accompanied them.

He shed a tear for Violet Florence Martin because he understood how sad it was to die with so many dreams unrealized. *What if?* is not the question with which to end your life, but the question with which to begin it.

Joseph told Violet to find her own way into the future, and she thanked him for listening and she went on her way.

When James arrived in the morning he told Joseph that the room felt different.

"Yes," Joseph said. "Violet has gone."

James wrote down everything that Joseph told him, and then he called his brother-in-law who was a junior reporter for *DublinObserver.com*. The brother-in-law was called Laurence Sterne. He had watched *All The President's Men* seven times and he wanted a scoop like Watergate. His hero was Bob Woodward and he was not ashamed to tell people.

That same afternoon, Laurence gave an account in the paper of the exorcism of a ghost at the Merrion Hotel by a guest called Joseph Conrad. Laurence gave the name of the deceased girl and the approximate date of her supposed death. It was a bit of fun really, and the tone of the piece was somewhere between dismissive and whimsical.

Three hundred and forty miles away, a man called Charles Maturin, a well-respected historian and a spiritualist of some renown, read that article and spilled his tea. He had heard of the *Merrion Girl*, as she was known in such circles, and this article – giving her name and the approximate date of her death – tallied precisely with two previous accounts. He e-mailed some colleagues. They e-mailed others. Within an hour a half there was a flurry of communications going back and forth about Joseph Conrad and the Merrion haunting.

Maturin called the Observer city desk. He was directed to Laurence Sterne.

"This Joseph Conrad...did you meet him?" Maturin asked.

"No, I did not. My brother-in-law gave me the information. He works at the Merrion."

"His name?"

"James Joyce."

"Like the novelist?"

"Yes. Spelled the same way exactly."

"Thank you, Mr. Sterne."

"You're welcome, Mr. Maturin."

Maturin then called the Merrion and asked for James Joyce.

"He is not here."

"By any chance, do you have a guest there by the name of Joseph Conrad?"

"One moment please, sir."

Maturin waited for a moment.

"Yes, sir."

"Oh, could you please try his room for me?"

Charles Maturin felt the flutter of butterflies in his stomach.

The phone rang. Once. Twice.

"Hello?"

"Mr. Conrad?"

"Yes, this is Mr. Conrad."

"Good day, sir. My names is Charles Maturin. I am a historian and a spiritualist, and I wondered if I might speak with you about the Violet Florence Martin case."

"She has gone. She left last night."

"So I understand, Mr. Conrad. I wondered if it might be possible to come to Ireland and discuss this with you, see the hotel room, talk about what happened."

"No, that won't be possible."

"I do appreciate your desire for privacy, Mr. Conrad. Especially when it comes to such matters - - "

"Such matters?"

"The gift, of course."

"The gift?"

"Yes, Mr. Conrad. I assume you have been employing your gift for some time."

"I don't really understand, Mr. Maturin. I listen to people when they talk. Sometimes those people don't have bodies any more and they are disturbed or frightened. I listen to them and they feel better and then they go on."

"Go on?"

"Yes, they go on... You know, they go and find another body or they do whatever they want to do. They don't have to stay where they were. It is usually the trauma that keeps them there, or that they just need someone to talk to. When they feel they have been heard they can let go. That's all."

Maturin cleared his throat. He sensed that this Joseph Conrad was something special. His manner was artless and lacked all contrivance. He spoke like a child.

"I really would like to come and talk with you, Mr. Conrad."

"I am sorry. I am leaving."

"Leaving Dublin?"

"I think I am leaving Ireland."

"And where are you going, and when?"

"I don't know, Mr. Maturin. Anyway, it was a pleasure to speak to you, and I hope you and your family are well, but I must go now because I am hungry."

There was a second's pause, and then Joseph said, 'Goodbye,' and hung up the phone.

Charles Maturin heard the line go dead and could scarcely recall a word of the conversation.

While on the telephone Joseph had been studying the room service menu. He dialed reception and asked for the roast rump of lamb with a brioche and thyme crust, buttered leeks, pea purée and herb mashed potato. The price was twenty-nine euros fifty, with a five-euro delivery charge.

The man asked if he would like something to drink.

"Some water," Joseph said. "Some fizzy water."

After Joseph had eaten, he tidied the room and checked to see that he had left nothing behind.

Downstairs he asked if they would call a taxi for him.

"The airport," Joseph said.

"You are leaving us?" the man asked. He had a concerned look on his face, as though something important would be missed if Joseph persisted with his wish to depart.

"It would seem so," Joseph said, and he smiled.

"And might we have the pleasure of your company again, sir?"

Joseph shook his head. "No."

"I am sorry to hear that, sir. I trust everything has been to your satisfaction."

"Yes, indeed. Everything has been excellent. I even spoke with your ghost, you know?"

"Yes, sir. It has been all over the internet. I must say that we have received an inordinate number of requests for reservations."

"Oh."

"Did you see your Facebook page, sir?"

Joseph frowned. "I don't have a Facebook page."

"Then someone must have made one for you. There are postings on there about the ghost, and apparently you were in France and you gave some money to some people."

"I was, and yes, I did."

"You have twelve thousand followers, sir…since I last checked."

"Twelve thousand people are following me?"

"I am sure it's a lot more than that now, sir."

Joseph glanced towards the front door of the building. "They're not outside, are they?"

The man laughed, and then he saw that Joseph was not laughing. "No sir, they're not outside."

"I find it hard to imagine twelve thousand people," Joseph said.

"Yes, sir. Now…you'd like to settle up. Could I have your card, please?"

"That won't be necessary."

A man that Joseph had not seen before appeared behind the first man. He smiled like a prizewinner. "I am the hotel manager," he said. "My name is Abraham Stoker." He stepped from around the desk and came towards Joseph. He extended his hand and Joseph met him half way. They shook hands and smiled at one another.

"You have created quite a little stir here, Mr. Conrad," Abraham Stoker said. "We have experienced an unprecedented number of bookings in the past few hours thanks to the article in the local paper. It appears to have gone viral on the internet."

"Oh," Joseph said. "I really am very sorry. I hope it will be okay."

Mr. Stoker laughed. "Quite the comedian, sir. Very amusing. So, as a token of our appreciation, we would like to waive your bill."

"Oh," Joseph said. "No, that wouldn't be right at all."

"I'm sorry, sir?"

"You have to pay for things. That's the way it works. If you take something and don't pay for it, that's stealing."

Stoker smiled, looked momentarily taken aback. "I'm not sure I understand, sir. We are merely gifting you your stay here as a thank you for the business you have generated."

Joseph nodded. "I know what you mean, Mr. Stoker, but that was not the agreement I made. The agreement I made was to take a room and pay for it. One should always maintain agreements."

"Yes, sir, of course, sir, but - - "

Joseph reached out and took Stoker's hand. He shook it again. "I really need to pay my bill and be on my way, Mr. Stoker," he said. "I have a taxi waiting."

"Very good, sir. Whatever you say."

10.

London was an unrelenting smash of humanity.

Alive, vital, energetic, frantic, even desperate, it ran at a phenomenal pace, but seemed to be uncertain of where it was going.

Joseph could feel the history of the place around every corner, beneath every eave, in every doorway, down every alleyway and street. People walked with mobile phones close to their faces, glancing up momentarily to ensure they didn't collide with one another. It was nothing less than a ballet, in equal parts elegance and ignorance.

Joseph wondered what would happen if the whole machine collapsed. Once upon a time there was no internet. It was intangible, ethereal, and those who used it did not even understand how it had been created. What would they think if it just wasn't there any more?

Such a thought made him smile.

He'd landed at Gatwick and taken a train to Victoria station. By the time he arrived it was dark and cold and there was a light mist of rain that made everything reflective.

Everywhere there were lights. Lights and people in a hurry. That's what the city appeared to be made of. He did not know where these people were going, but it was evidently very important. He returned to the underground and he took several trains just to see where they arrived. Seven Sisters was one place, because the name intrigued him, and then he got off and took another train back towards the river. Then out again on a different train. Random journeys.

In Bethnal Green, a young man asked Joseph if he had any money.

"Yes, I do."

"Give me some, mister," he said.

"How much do you need and what is it for?"

"Twenty quid. So I can get some food, sleep in a hostel maybe."

"Are you hungry?"

"Starving."

"You must be cold as well."

"Freezing."

"Do you not have an overcoat?"

"No mate, I don't."

Joseph took off his coat. The one he'd bought at Arnott's. "Here," he said. "There's money in the pocket."

The young man smiled awkwardly. "What is this?"

"It's just a coat," Joseph said.

"Are we on TV? Is there a hidden camera somewhere?"

Joseph didn't say anything. He just held the coat out and smiled.

"What is going on here?" the young man said. "You want me to blow you or something?"

"I want you to take the coat and the money and get something to eat and find somewhere to sleep, and then I think you should call your father and go home. Like Emily did."

The young man looked at Joseph. He reached out tentatively, perhaps expecting the coat to be whipped away. It was not.

"Thanks, mister," he said, and whatever self-defence and disbelief was in his voice was no longer there.

"You're welcome," Joseph said, and then a train pulled into the station and Joseph got on it and sat down.

Before the doors closed the young man leaned in and said, "What's your name?"

"Conrad," Joseph said. "My name is Joseph Conrad."

Joseph travelled to Covent Garden. When he got there, he saw no garden. There were buildings, and a fountain where people sat and talked and smoked and talked some more. Other people were laughing and drinking wine and they seemed happy.

There was a hotel that went by the same name, and Joseph liked how it looked and it seemed to be old and have an atmosphere. There were two young men inside, and they opened the doors for Joseph and greeted him enthusiastically.

"Good evening, sir," they said, both of them at the same time, and it was a stereo welcome.

"Good evening," Joseph said. "My name is Joseph Conrad, and I would like to stay here."

The young man on the left wore a badge on his waistcoat that said *Nathan*. The one on the left was *Oscar*. Nathan directed Joseph toward the reception desk, and a pretty woman with a badge that said *Elizabeth* smiled and welcomed Joseph and asked him how she could help.

"I want a room," Joseph said. "What do you recommend?"

"Will sir be staying alone?"

"Yes."

"And does sir know how long he will be staying?"

"No, he doesn't," Joseph replied, wondering for a moment why they kept referring to him in the third person when he was standing right there.

"Does sir have any preference? Perhaps a double room, a suite, a loft, a four poster room?"

"What's that?"

"The four poster room, sir?"

"Yes."

"It's a room with a four poster bed, sir."

"Yes," Joseph said. "I have never slept in one of those. I shall take that room."

"Yes, of course, sir," Elizabeth said, and Joseph could tell from her eyes that she was anxious about many things, and none of them were very important.

Joseph smiled as Elizabeth tapped on a keyboard, and then he asked if she knew Charles Bukowski.

"No, sir," she replied. "I don't know anyone called Charles Bukowski."

"Charles Bukowski was a writer," Joseph explained. "He was a writer and a poet and a subversive and a drunk. He was a man of mighty intellect and mightier contradictions. He knew how to live life, and he knew what it was to be alone. His poetry sings clear and brilliant with extraordinary human choruses that resonate with anyone who has ever lived, loved or lost."

Elizabeth looked up at Joseph. A nerve was clearly exposed.

"A love like that was a serious illness," Joseph quoted, "an illness from which you never entirely recover."

Elizabeth laughed, but beneath that laugh was a shadow of grief.

"Pain is strange," he went on. "A cat killing a bird, a car accident, a fire. Pain arrives. Bang! And there it is. It sits on you. It's real. And to anybody watching, you look foolish. Like you've suddenly become an idiot. There's no cure for it unless you know somebody who understands how you feel, and knows how to help."

"Do you know how to help, Mr. Conrad?"

"Perhaps, but I think Mr. Bukowski knows how to help best."

"And what would Mr. Bukowski say?"

"There's nothing to mourn about death any more than there is to mourn about the growing of a flower. What is terrible is not death but the lives people live or don't live up until their death. Soon they forget how to think. They let others think for them. Their brains are stuffed with cotton. They look ugly, they talk ugly, they walk ugly. Play them the great music of the centuries and they can't hear it. Most people's deaths are a sham. There's nothing left to die."

"Sometimes I feel like I am in a dream," Elizabeth said.

"We don't even ask for happiness…just for a little less pain."

Her eyes widened. "I am not even alive most of the time, am I? That's how it feels."

"We are here to laugh at the odds and live our lives so well that Death will tremble to take us."

"He told me to go with him, and I was afraid," she said.

"I understand fear," Joseph said.

"I read that thing once…something like most of your problems would be solved with twenty seconds of courage."

"Some of us run from rain but sit in bathtubs of water."

"It was stupid, wasn't it? Being so afraid. All he did was ask me to go with him. I mean, it wasn't even a different country or anything. It was Manchester."

Joseph said nothing.

"I have spent a week crying and convincing myself that I made the right decision not to go. He texts me. He begs me to change my mind. What am I fighting?"

Again, Joseph said nothing.

"I miss him so terribly."

"Perhaps you should talk to him, Elizabeth."

She looked up at Joseph. There were tears in her eyes. Her mascara was smudged and it gave her a bruised and fragile appearance.

"Look at me," she said, and laughed again. "I must look a mess." She fingertipped her tears away and smudged her mascara further.

"Who cares how you look?" he said. "Better to look a fool than act as one."

"I am supposed to be booking your room."

"I'll take the four poster, as agreed."

77

Elizabeth completed the booking and swiped Joseph's card.

"I am so sorry," she said, handing him the room key. "So very unprofessional of me…sharing my personal problems with a guest."

Joseph smiled. "For fear of talking to one another, perhaps we should stay silent and suffer for ever?"

"You are very kind," she said. She looked at Joseph, as if for the first time, and he reminded her so very much of Jamie Bell. She did like Jamie Bell so very much.

"I am just like everyone else," Joseph replied.

A bellhop appeared. "You have luggage, sir?"

"No," Joseph said. "I always feel it's better to travel light."

The room was ideal, as was the bed. Joseph lay on it and imagined he was King Henry VIII.

He hoped Elizabeth would call the man in Manchester and go to him. It would be the right thing to do for both of them. There was little worse than the knowledge of absence.

Joseph was hungry, but he did not want to eat in the hotel. He wanted to see more lights and more hurrying people.

He went downstairs and walked through reception. Nathan and Oscar opened the door for him and wished him a cheery *Good evening!*

Elizabeth was nowhere to be seen.

11.

The young man stood quietly at the side of the railway line. He had already decided that today was the day he would die.

He was no more than twenty-three or twenty-four, and his heart was broken in too many places for it ever to mend. Neither glue nor stitches nor splints nor plasters nor love could make the necessary repairs, and so he would go.

How he would go he had not fully decided. Stepping in front of the very next train was an option, but that was all it was. It was a simple matter of knowing that today was *the* day. Details were secondary.

The young man was alone and Joseph did not wish to say a word until his voice was the only sound to be heard.

Dogs barked.

In the distance children ran and laughed and played and cried.

Somewhere a siren wailed, as if mimicking the grief that would be discovered at its destination.

"Emily told me that sometimes we take the wrong road to get to the right place," Joseph eventually said. His voice was calm and measured.

The man looked up. "Who the hell is Emily?"

"A girl I met in Paris who was being a prostitute."

"Right," the young man said.

"May I stand beside you?" Joseph asked.

"Free country, isn't it?" the young man replied.

"No, I don't believe it is. Very far from it, as far as I can see."

Joseph's comment coaxed the ghost of a smile from the young man.

"I know how to be alone, how to hurt this much; to stand beneath the closing day, unknown, unloved, untouched. Pieces of the man I was, scattered on the ground; they fell apart so gracefully, I never heard a sound."

"What's that? A poem?"

"Maybe," Joseph said. "Perhaps a song. I just wrote it for you."

"You a nutcase or what? You're not one of those God-botherers, are you?"

"I have no idea what a God-botherer is, but I saw you here and I thought of a few words to share with you that I knew you would understand."

"Unheard, unloved…" the man said.

"Untouched," Joseph added.

"It's a mess, you know?"

"I know."

"It's a wretched, filthy, desperate mess and I can't do anything about it."

"I know. We never can."

"Then what the hell is the point?" the man asked.

"What's your name?"

"Aldous. Aldous Huxley."

Joseph extended his hand. "My name is Joseph Conrad."

There was silence for a moment.

"How will you do it?" Joseph asked.

"Do what?"

"End this wretched, filthy, desperate mess. Are you going to step in front of the train?"

"The train, maybe. Or jump off the bridge."

"Which train? What time, do you think?"

"Does it matter?"

"Not to you, no. Any train will be fine. The next one, the one after. They will all accomplish the same end. I was thinking more about the people who need to get home and feed their children, the ones who are rushing to deal with an emergency, the ones with sick relatives. That kind of thing. You end a life under a train, but how many other lives are affected in ways you could never imagine, I wonder…"

"What do I care about other people?"

"Yes," Joseph said. "Good point."

"And what the hell do you care anyway? What business is it of yours?"

"None of my business," Joseph said.

"Well good. Then we don't have a problem, do we?"

"No. No, we don't."

Joseph looked up at the sky and sighed.

"What? You're just gonna go on standing there?" Aldous asked.

"Free country."

Aldous laughed. "No actually, I don't think it is."

Joseph nodded in agreement.

"Everyone is a mess," Aldous said. "Never met anyone who knew what the hell was really going on. People just stumble through life and never open their eyes and they keep on making the same mistakes, don't they?"

"Yes, they do. I see that very clearly."

"I mean, seriously - - "

"I wouldn't do that if I were you," Joseph interjected.

Aldous frowned. "Do what?"

"Take anything seriously."

"You have to take things seriously."

"Well, if you say so. But we will have to agree to disagree."

"What are you talking about? Life is serious. Life is really serious. Serious stuff happens all the time."

"Yes, I guess it appears serious for a while. And then it happens and you look back and it seems nowhere as serious as before." Joseph nodded his head slowly. "Like exams at school. Like your first sweetheart. Like your driving test. All very serious and important, all very life-or-death until after they're gone, and then they seem like nothing at all."

Aldous was quiet for a moment. "Yeah," he said.

"Do you want to hear something? It's a theory I have. Something I've been thinking about for a while."

"Sure, whatever."

"So we have a problem in our life. Something doesn't go well, something happens. It's a bad situation and it's going to take some work to sort it out. Maybe it's a long-term thing, or maybe it's something that happened out-of-the-blue. Whatever it is, we're standing there looking at this problem and we know we have to deal with it. You understand?"

"Sure. Yeah."

"Okay, so then we decide not to handle it right now. We push it over to one side. We tell ourselves we don't have to fix it all at once, that it can wait. Or maybe we just convince ourselves that it's not such a big deal, that it will sort itself out, you know? Time, after all, is the Great Healer."

Aldous smiled knowingly.

"So it sits there. It doesn't go away. It's the last thing we think of when we go to sleep, the first thing we think of when we wake up in the morning. It doesn't vanish by magic, and it certainly doesn't look like anyone is going to fix it for us."

Aldous didn't say a word.

"And you know what happens…we wind up having to deal with it ourselves anyway. And you know what else? That problem looks bigger now. It has sharper teeth. Why? Because the fact that we didn't deal with it the first time around made us weaker. We go to battle the second time, and already we are carrying the burden of knowledge. We let ourselves down. We didn't fight the dragon. We didn't even draw our sword." Joseph shrugged. "I mean, I don't know if that's true or not. Like I said, it was just an idea."

"It's a good idea, Joseph," Aldous said.

"You think so?"

"Sure. It's a good idea. I guess it always makes sense to deal with it when it happens, but there's a universe of differences between good ideas and the real world."

"Yes," Joseph said. "There is. An idea is only so useful as it works."

"I appreciate you coming to talk to me."

"But the road to Hell is paved with good intentions."

"I don't think you can do anything to help me, man."

"Okay," Joseph replied.

"I mean, what the hell could you do? You don't even know what the problem is…" Aldous laughed dismissively. "Problem. Jesus Christ. *Problem.* I have a hundred problems."

"Yes. A hundred problems."

84

"I mean, just for starters, my girlfriend slept with some other guy - - "

"I don't think that was the first problem," Joseph said.

Aldous hesitated. "What are you, man? Are you like a Samaritan or something?"

Joseph shook his head. "No," he said. "I am just unemployed."

Aldous laughed. "Join the club."

"You lost your job?"

"Lost my job, lost my girlfriend, lost my flat."

"You've lost a lot."

"Everything."

"You didn't lose your life."

"No. Not yet."

"But you want to?"

Aldous turned and looked at Joseph. "I want to lose the life that I have now."

"Or maybe you just want to change it?"

"Yes."

"To what? What kind of life do you want?"

"The life where I have a flat and a girlfriend and a job."

"You had those things and you lost them."

"Yes. I screwed up. I screwed up so bad."

"Like the rest of us. I think it's called being human."

"Being human sucks."

"Yes."

"So what the hell do I do, Joseph?"

"You find a reason, Aldous."

"Yes."

"A reason for what?"

"Just a reason to still be here tomorrow - - "

"Hey! Hey, what are you guys doing?"

Joseph and Aldous turned in the same moment.

A policeman with a hard face was walking towards them, behind him a Community Support Officer.

"Get away from that rail line," the policeman said. "Get away from the railway line right now."

Both Aldous and Joseph stepped back together as one.

"What are you doing here?" the policeman asked. The nametag on his stab jacket said *Orwell*. The PCSO's name was *Heyer*.

"Talking," Joseph said.

Orwell looked at Aldous. "Was this man harassing you, sir?"

Aldous laughed. "You are harassing me."

Orwell scowled. He looked at Heyer. Heyer scowled too.

"I don't believe I am doing anything of the sort, sir," Orwell said. His manner was formalized and unnatural, as if he had been told to use those precise words and none other.

"I believe you are interfering with law-abiding citizens who are engaged in nothing more suspicious than a conversation," Aldous said.

"I don't appreciate your tone," PCSO Heyer said.

"I don't give a damn whether you appreciate my tone or not," Aldous replied.

"Okay, sir," Orwell said, a look in his eye that was somehow vindictive. "I have reason to suspect that you may be carrying controlled substances."

Aldous laughed. "Go to Hell."

Orwell gave his name and the police station he was from; he then moved toward Aldous and asked him to raise his arms so his pockets could be searched.

"You're not searching me," Aldous said.

"Yes, sir. I have the right to search you if I believe that you are carrying an illegal substance."

"I refuse your rights," Aldous said. "What is this, a police state?"

"You have to cooperate," Heyer said.

Joseph took a step backward.

"Please don't go anywhere, sir," Heyer warned him. "You're involved in this."

Joseph smiled. "Involved in what?"

She gave him a superficial and knowing smile, but did not further any explanation.

Orwell took another step toward Aldous. He reached out and held Aldous's arm. Aldous shrugged it away.

"Don't touch me, man. What the hell is this?"

"I have the right to search you, sir. You must cooperate, or I will be forced to arrest you."

Aldous did not cooperate.

Orwell arrested him.

Heyer took Joseph's arm and said, "You better come along, sir. Just until we sort out exactly what has been going on here."

"I think you'll find it was just a conversation," Joseph said.

"Let us do our job, sir," Heyer replied.

"What job is that?" Joseph asked.

"Keeping the peace, sir," Heyer replied. "Protecting innocent civilians."

"From what?" Joseph asked.

"Move along, sir," Heyer said, and she urged him forward with her hand.

12.

Joseph sat quietly for a long time, it seemed. But time was elastic and fragile, and sometimes it took different shapes and forms, and one could never be absolutely sure that a minute was really a minute, or if it was something else.

It was a similar scenario to the one in France, he imagined.

After another indefinite lapse, the door opened in the small white room into which he'd been directed.

A man looked at him for a second as if unsure that he was meant to be there, and then he smiled and closed the door behind him.

"Hello," Joseph said.

"Good day, sir," the man replied. "I am Sergeant Dylan Thomas."

"I am Joseph Conrad."

Sergeant Thomas sat facing Joseph. He placed a thin manila folder on the table.

"Did anyone offer you a cup of tea, sir?"

"No," Joseph said. "Were they supposed to?"

Sergeant Thomas opened the folder. There was a single sheet of paper.

"It appears that you have been brought to the station without due cause, sir," the sergeant explained.

"Oh," Joseph replied.

"According to the information that we have secured from Mr. Huxley, you were merely a bystander."

"An innocent bystander," Joseph said, and smiled.

"Sorry sir?"

"It's a wine that I drank above a bookshop in Dublin," Joseph said. "Selina recommended it."

"Selina?"

"She worked in the restaurant."

"And what does she have to do with Mr. Huxley?"

"I have no idea, Sergeant Thomas," Joseph said. "Does she know him?"

"We will ask him," the sergeant said, and he jotted a few words on his piece of paper.

He looked up again. "So, as I was saying, it appears you were brought here without due cause."

Joseph didn't reply.

"Mr. Huxley said that you and he are not known to one another."

"I know him as well as I know anyone."

Sergeant Thomas frowned. "That appears to conflict with the information we have secured, sir."

"Who really *knows* anyone?" Joseph said.

"So you and he are not friends?"

"I would say we are. Acquaintances, friends, fellow human beings. We had a conversation this morning about whether he would jump under a train or off a bridge."

"And this was your first meeting with Mr. Huxley?"

"I had not seen him before today."

The sergeant nodded. "Good. Okay. Now I understand. Okay so he also told us that you spoke to him and convinced him not to jump under the train or off a bridge. Is that so?"

"No, I don't believe I convinced him of anything."

"I am confused."

Joseph smiled understandingly. "Sometimes I get confused too."

"So, did you or did you not talk him out of committing suicide, Mr. Conrad?"

"I listened to him. That was all I did. I don't think he really planned to end his life. I think he just needed someone to listen to him. To hear what he had to say, you know?"

"Yes, sir."

"So I stood there and listened to him and then those people came and they brought us here without due cause. I think the man...his name is Orwell, yes? I think he is very angry about things. He is not happy in his life."

Thomas shook is head resignedly. "Who is these days?"

"I am asking myself the same question," Joseph said.

"So you were nothing but a good Samaritan, it seems."

"I am many things, Sergeant Thomas."

Thomas was about to close his manila folder and he hesitated.

"Are you alright, sir?"

"Why do you ask?"

"Nothing, really. It's just that you seem...I don't know, sir. I have to be honest and say that this is not the sort of conversation I am used to."

"And what kind of conversations are you used to?"

Thomas laughed a little. "I don't know, sir. This doesn't really seem like a normal conversation."

"Oh."

"Might I ask where you live, sir?"

"I don't live anywhere."

"You're homeless?"

"For now, yes."

"And where are you from?"

"Originally?"

"Yes, sir. Where are you from originally?"

Joseph looked up at the ceiling. "I don't really know, to be honest."

"Well, where were you born?"

"I don't remember."

"You don't remember where you were born?"

"No. Do you?"

"Yes. Yes, of course I remember."

"You remember, or someone told you?"

Thomas looked awkward for a moment. "Your parents are alive, sir?"

"I don't know."

"You were orphaned, adopted, fostered, taken into care, perhaps?"

"I have no idea, Sergeant Thomas."

"So you have no home, you don't know where you're from, and you have no idea who your parents are?"

"Is there a problem?"

Sergeant Thomas smiled. "It's a little unusual, Mr. Conrad."

"Is there a problem with being unusual?"

"Well, sir, it isn't a matter of what I think, it's a matter of what others might think."

"I disagree."

"I'm sorry?"

"I disagree with what you just said. I think it's nearly always about what you think, and very rarely about what others think. From what

I have seen so far, it appears that worrying about what other people think is the most pointless and popular pastime of this civilization."

Sergeant Thomas picked up the file and rose to his feet. "Before you go, sir, I think it might be a good idea for you to have a few words with someone else, if that's okay?"

"I am happy to talk to anyone," Joseph said.

"Very good, sir. It won't be long."

"One question, Sergeant Thomas."

"Yes, sir."

"What is a controlled substance?"

"Oh, that's just a term we use to mean illegal drugs and suchlike."

"Mr. Orwell suspected Aldous had some controlled substances, and that was why he wanted to search him. Did he have any?"

"No, sir, I don't believe he did."

"And where is he now?"

"Mr. Huxley or Constable Orwell?"

"Aldous. Where is Aldous?"

"I think he has been released, sir."

"Oh," Joseph said. "Okay."

Sergeant Thomas hesitated for one moment more, and then he smiled uncomfortably and left the room.

13.

Another man entered the room. Beneath his arm he carried his own manila folder, and in each hand he carried a cup of tea. He opened and closed the door with his elbow, and he spilled a little tea on his shoe. The shoe was suede and he seemed quite irritated.

"Sorry," he said, even though it was not Joseph's shoe. "Clumsy."

The man brought the tea to the table. He set a cup down in front of Joseph.

"Tea," he said.

Joseph nodded. "Yes."

"I didn't know if you took sugar," the man said.

"No."

The man smiled. "Good. Excellent. There's no sugar in it."

The man sat down. He put his manila folder on the table and took a pen from his pocket. He opened the folder and looked carefully at the single sheet of paper within. He read down the notes, using the pen along the margin to follow what he was reading. After a very short while he looked up and smiled.

"My name is Doctor Samuel Johnson," he said.

"I am Joseph Conrad," Joseph said.

"I know," Dr. Johnson said. "It gives your name here."

"Yes."

"I am a police psychologist," Dr. Johnson explained. "Do you know what that is?"

"You study the souls of policemen," Joseph replied. "*Psyche* is Greek for soul and *ology* means study of."

Dr. Johnson smiled. "Sadly no," he said. He leaned forward fractionally, his voice lowered as if relaying a conspiratorial message. "Though I wouldn't be surprised to find out that most of these coppers here don't have a soul."

"Oh," Joseph replied.

The doctor seemed to be waiting for some other response.

"So you don't study the human soul?" Joseph asked.

"Er…no, no we don't."

"Then why do you call yourself a psychologist?"

"Well, it's a little more complicated than that, Joseph."

Joseph smiled. "I am beginning to understand that this is one of the things people say when they don't really want to answer the question - - "

"Well, you see - - "

"Or they don't know the answer to the question."

The doctor leaned back in his chair. He sipped his tea. He seemed to be uncertain of what to say next.

"Have you ever been interviewed by a psychiatrist or psychologist, Joseph?"

"No Samuel, I have not."

"I would prefer it if you would call me Dr. Johnson."

"You don't like Samuel. It's a good name. It's a very old name."

"No, I am fine with Samuel, but for the purposes of this interview I feel it best if we maintain a degree of formality."

"Very well, Dr. Johnson."

"So, Joseph - - "

"Mr. Conrad."

The doctor paused. He smiled as if understanding something deeply profound.

"So, Mr. Conrad," he began again, "have you ever been interviewed by a psychiatrist or psychologist?"

"No, Dr. Johnson. As far as I am aware, you are the first."

"You have never been admitted to a psychiatric clinic or institutional facility? You have never been admitted to the psychiatric wing of a hospital?"

"Not to my knowledge."

"Are you currently taking any prescription medication?"

"No."

"Are you currently taking any other drugs, legal or otherwise?"

"You mean like a controlled substance?"

"Yes, exactly."

"No."

"Very well," the doctor said, and he made a series of cryptic notes on his page. "So, please tell me what happened this morning…the incident with Mr. Huxley at the train station."

"Mr. Huxley and I engaged in a pleasant conversation, and then the two police people came and they got angry and they threatened Mr. Huxley and then they arrested him."

"Because Constable Orwell suspected Mr. Huxley was in possession of controlled substances."

"No, I don't think so," Joseph replied.

"Oh, what do you think happened?"

"I think Mr. Huxley's attitude threatened Constable Orwell's belief in his own superiority, and Constable Orwell became defensive and insecure and he exerted his control on the situation the only way he could.

96

He used the symbolism of the police force to establish his authority in an effort to prove to himself and Mr. Huxley that he was actually in charge. He also wanted to impress the woman."

Dr. Johnson raised his eyebrows and smiled in a condescending manner.

"And now you are going to tell me that you are the only person qualified to give an opinion as to the state of mind and rationale of people," Joseph said.

Dr. Johnson became visibly flustered.

"And now you are going to tell me that you were not thinking that," Joseph added.

"Mr. Conrad - - "

"Yes, Dr. Johnson."

"I am not accustomed to finding people this combative."

"Okay."

"You agree you are being combative."

"I have not agreed anything."

Johnson smiled. He tucked the single sheet of paper in the folder and folded his hands together on the table. He then changed his mind and drank some more tea.

"I think it best we begin again, Mr. Conrad."

Joseph said nothing. The doctor's mental machinery was noisy, disturbingly so. He seemed to be in some desperate battle with himself. He seemed to be confused about many things.

"All that we are trying to establish here, Mr. Conrad, is whether or not you are in a potentially…shall we say, a *challenged* situation?"

"Challenged by what, Dr. Johnson?"

"Well, you have indicated that you are without a job, without a home, that you do not remember where you were born, nor do you have any information about your parents, and we feel that there is perhaps some indication of a...well, what we call a *learning disability*..."

"What is it that I have been unable to learn?" Joseph asked.

Johnson smiled again. "Well, it is not that simple."

"Oh, I see," Joseph replied. "It seems that you live in a very complicated world, Dr. Johnson."

"The brain is a complicated thing, Mr. Conrad."

"The brain is a complicated thing."

"Yes, very complicated."

"I tend not to use it for much," Joseph said. "Physiological monitoring, cellular processes, glandular secretions and inhibitions, maintaining internal temperature, muscular communications...the whole central nervous system kind of machinery and management, you know?"

"And all your mental processes, of course - - "

"No. I use my mind for that."

Johnson laughed. "The mind and the brain are quite the same thing, Mr. Conrad."

"Oh," Joseph replied, and he smiled as if he now understood.

"What?" Johnson asked.

"I was wondering why you were so confused, why your life was so fantastically complicated, Dr. Johnson. Now I think I understand."

"You are telling me that you understand more about the brain and the mind than myself?"

"I didn't say anything like that."

"But you are implying it?"

"I have implied nothing."

"I'll have you know that I have been a practicing psychologist for over twenty years. I have been published in numerous journals and pamphlets. I graduated with honours from a very prestigious university indeed."

Joseph didn't reply.

"And I must say I find your dismissive attitude quite insulting, Mr. Conrad."

"Okay."

"I have no choice but to recommend that some sort of official supervision or surveillance be maintained until we get to the bottom of this."

"The bottom of what, Dr. Johnson?"

"What you were doing on a train track this morning. Why you have no home, no recollection of family - - "

"Have I broken the law, Dr. Johnson?"

"Not to my knowledge, no."

"Have I hurt someone?"

"Not that I am aware of, no."

"Do you have any legal right to detain me?"

"I am a qualified police psychologist, and that empowers me to direct the detention of any individual I believe might pose a threat to themselves or the community at large."

"Oh," Joseph said.

Johnson stood up. He collected his cup, his folder and his pen, and he walked to the door.

He once again attempted to open the door with his elbow, and once again spilled a few drops of tea on his suede loafer.

"Oh bollocks," he mumbled, and manoeuvered his way out of the room without looking back at Joseph.

14.

It had rained quite heavily during the night, and it was still raining in the morning. Nevertheless, Aldous Huxley was outside with two journalists and a girl from a local radio station. The station was called *Life FM*. The girl was called Virginia Woolf.

According to the duty sergeant Aldous had come back the previous evening asking for Joseph. He had been informed that Joseph was being held for *further observation*. Aldous had demanded more information. The officer on duty had not been willing to give him any more information. Aldous had gone away and come back with the press. He had told them that he was a potential suicide, that Joseph had offered assistance – a good Samaritan – and that the police now considered him a risk to public safety. Why else would they detain him? It was a scandal. They were going to talk about it on the radio. Both of the journalists were planning to write something in the newspaper.

All of this was explained to Joseph by a Police Public Relations Coordinator called Isabella Banks.

"We don't really understand what happened," Isabella told Joseph. "You really shouldn't have been held here overnight."

"I was being observed," Joseph said.

"Yes, apparently so, but Dr. Johnson didn't appear to have sufficient grounds to order such a detention."

"He wanted to make sure I did not pose a threat to myself or the community at large."

100

"Yes, I understand. There are many provisions under the Mental Health Act to detain someone for observational purposes, but in such instances it is necessary to have medical and psychiatric records available, even to seek the opinion of a second physician or psychiatrist."

"I think he was upset because I mentioned the souls of police officers, and because of the tea on his shoes."

Isabella Banks frowned for a moment, and then she smiled like she really meant it. There was something strangely charming about the young man. Aside from that, he looked like Benedict Cumberbatch and that could never be a bad thing.

"I don't know what else to tell you, Mr. Conrad. All I can do is extend my sincerest apologies for the way you have been treated, and assure you that we will cooperate with you in every way possible to ensure that adequate restitution for your inconvenience is afforded."

"Restitution?"

"If you claim damages, Mr. Conrad."

Joseph smiled. "Damages for what, Miss Banks?"

"For the unlawful detention, the way in which you have been treated - - "

"I have been treated with nothing but courtesy, Miss Banks. I stayed in a warm room. They brought me some dinner. I had a cup of tea."

"They put you in a cell, Joseph."

"Yes, it was quiet. I slept very well."

Isabella Banks seemed a little bemused. "You certainly seem to be taking this very well, Joseph. Are you saying that you have no intention of pursuing a formal complaint against the Police?"

"I have no complaint with anyone, Isabella."

Her relief was visible. She confirmed Joseph's observation by saying, "I am so relieved." Then she said, "It seems to be the slightest thing, these days. Everyone is so aggressive and litigious."

"Yes," Joseph replied. "A while ago people started to think that the reason for their troubles was other people and not themselves."

Isabella smiled. "I think it's a little more complicated than that."

"Oh," Joseph said. "I don't."

Outside the rain was consistent but light. It moistened everything.

Virginia Woolf had a small hand-held digital recorder and she was asking questions one after the other.

"Is it true that you recently exorcised a ghost from a hotel room in Dublin, Mr. Conrad? Are you the same Joseph Conrad who gave money to a couple in France? Did you pay the airfare of a woman called Emily so she could return home from Paris? Did you know that you have over sixty thousand followers on Facebook, Mr. Conrad?"

Joseph didn't say anything.

"Leave him be," Aldous said, and then he looked at Joseph and there was something altogether hungry about him. "We need to get you out of here. You need to talk to these people, but not outside the police station."

Aldous led the way. Virginia Woolf and the two journalists followed him. Joseph followed on afterward.

"Are you making a political statement?" the younger journalist asked. "Is this perhaps some sort of social commentary, Mr. Conrad?"

His name was Anthony Burgess, and all five of them sat in a conference room in a hotel a few streets from the police station.

"About what?" Joseph asked.

The other journalist leaned forward eagerly. His name was Ian Fleming. "About the state of society, you know? You are making a statement about society with these acts of generosity...how people have lost sight of one another, of their own humanity, how it's all about fifteen minutes of fame and superficial celebrity, and everyone has forgotten what it is to be selfless and humanitarian."

"If you say so," Joseph said, and smiled.

Burgess and Fleming wrote things down. Virginia Woolf checked that her recorder was working for the third time.

"So, do you hope that the you will inspire some sort of movement, Mr. Conrad?" Virginia asked. "That people will follow your example?"

"People should do what they feel is right for them and the people they care for," Joseph said. "It is not my job to tell people how to live their lives. I don't believe it's anyone's job to tell people how to live their lives."

"Yes, yes, yes," Ian Fleming said. "So this is a rebellion against the nanny state, the relentless interference of government in our personal lives?"

"Of course it is," Aldous interjected. "This is a bloodless protest against tyranny, against the slow and insidious withdrawal of our fundamental human rights...the way that society has stripped us of our individuality and made us unthinking robots. Like reality TV. Like all these dancing and cooking and decorating programs. As if anyone really gives a damn about these things!"

"Is that so, Mr. Conrad?" Burgess asked. "Is that what this is all about?"

"I don't know what you mean, Mr. Burgess," Joseph said. "I just liked the idea of...I don't know, some acts of kindness perhaps."

"And is there any system or method to these *acts of kindness*, Mr. Conrad? I mean, why France? Why French people? Why Dublin?"

"I had never been there," Joseph said. "I wanted to see those places."

"So there is no itinerary here, no preordained plan of action?"

"No," Joseph replied. "I just go where I want to go."

"Random," Fleming said.

"There are always surprises," Joseph said. "Life may be inveterately grim and the surprises disproportionately unpleasant, but it would be hardly worth living if there were no exceptions, no sunny days, no acts of random kindness." He nodded in affirmation. "TC Boyle said that."

"Random acts of kindness," Burgess echoed.

"Yes," Ian Fleming said, and wrote it down.

"Yes, yes," Virginia Woolf said. "Simple. Succinct. Powerful. It says it all."

"So, about this police mistreatment," Burgess said. "Are you filing a formal complaint? Are you suing the police for - - "

"No," Joseph said. "I am not making any complaints, and I am not suing anyone."

"What the hell?" Aldous said. "You have to, man. Strike at the heart of the beast."

Joseph frowned. "There is a beast?"

"You know what I mean, man. Take 'em. Take 'em for all you can. You gotta make some money out of this."

"I don't need any money," Joseph said.

"You are a man of independent wealth?" Miss Woolf asked.

"I have my redundancy money. That is enough."

"So you had a job?" Fleming asked.

"Yes, I did."

"Who did you work for?"

"I worked for Menella," Joseph said.

"Hold up a minute," Aldous said, his voice sharp and percussive. "We're getting off the track here. We're talking about filing a complaint against the police, about getting some money."

Joseph turned and looked at Aldous. "If you need some money, I can give you some."

"I'm not talking about me, Joseph, I'm talking about you."

"I already said that I have no complaint, I am not suing anyone, and I don't need any money."

"This is crazy," Aldous said. "No one has enough money. Not even the richest guy in the world has enough money."

Virginia Woolf and the two journalists looked at Aldous Huxley.

"What?" Aldous said. "Are you stupid, or what? He could make a load of money here."

"Didn't you hear what he said?" Burgess asked. "He said it wasn't about the money."

"You people are crazy," Aldous said. He got up from the chair and pushed it noisily against the edge of the table. "It's always about the money."

He walked towards the door, hesitated before opening it, and said, "I don't even know why I told you people about this. You've all completely missed the point."

With that he opened the door, stepped out, and slammed it behind him.

"So, Mr. Conrad," Fleming said. "Tell us what you plan to do now?"

"Have some lunch, I think" Joseph said.

Fleming laughed. "Funny. Funny guy. So deadpan."

"We meant as far as this…this whole thing is concerned," Virginia Woolf said. "The next step in your project."

"I have no project," Joseph said. "I will just get some lunch."

With that, he rose slowly from the chair, smiled at each of them in turn, and said, "It was a pleasure to meet you all."

As Joseph left the room he closed the door very gently behind him.

The three journalists looked at each other in turn, but not one of them said a word.

Life FM ran a short human interest piece in their six o'clock news bulletin.

Both the journalists posted a squib in their on-line blog.

By eighty-thirty that same evening the number of people following Joseph Conrad had risen to ninety-four and a half thousand.

Random Acts of Kindness had become the buzzword.

On Twitter, people were talking about having some tee-shirts made up.

15.

"I like to read," Joseph said. "For as long as I can remember I have been reading. I don't know how many books I have read. I did start counting, but then it seemed to serve no purpose. I remember that it was more than a thousand, and then it didn't seem to matter any more. I just kept on reading anyway."

The girl in Foyles smiled and put Joseph's copy of Cocteau's *The Difficulty of Being* in a bag.

"I don't need a bag," Joseph said, and the girl took the book out and handed it over.

"You must love books too," he said. He looked at her name-badge. "Annie."

"Yes," she said. " I do."

"My name is Joseph Conrad," Joseph said, and he handed Annie his bankcard.

"Like the novelist," Annie said. She swiped the card.

"Exactly the same," Joseph replied.

She returned Joseph's card, and even as she did so a flicker of curiosity crossed her brow. A cloud shadow on a field.

"You're not *the* Joseph Conrad, are you?" Annie asked.

"I am the only one I know," he said.

"I mean...*the* Joseph Conrad, the one that's been on the radio...the one that's got that mad viral thing going on on the net?"

Joseph didn't know what to say, and so he said nothing.

"You know a guy called Aldous Huxley, right?"

Joseph smiled. "I met him, yes. At the train station."

"You *are* the guy," Annie said, her eyes wide. "He said that you saved his life. And you gave that money to those French people. It's all over the net." She looked around as if seeking out someone to tell. "Wow," she said. "Wow. Oh, wow." She seemed flustered. "Can I take a picture of you? No, better still…can I have a picture with you? Would that be okay?"

Joseph shrugged. "I have no camera."

"On my phone," Annie said. She waved at a colleague.

"Christine…this is Joseph Conrad. *The* Joseph Conrad."

Christine seemed stunned. "No way."

"Yes way," Annie replied. "Take my photo…quick, before Dorothy comes."

Annie came from behind the till. She stood next to Joseph. She put her hand through the crook of his elbow and pulled him close.

Joseph smiled. Her hair smelled like Charlotte's.

"Now me…me too," Christine said, and Annie took her picture with Joseph.

"Can we post these?" Christine asked. "Is it okay if we post them?"

"To whom?" Joseph asked.

Christine laughed. "On the net. Can we post them on the net?"

"Whatever you like," Joseph said.

The excitement seemed to be over then. He looked at Annie, then at Christine, and it seemed neither of them had anything else to say.

Joseph picked up his book from the counter near the till.

"Goodbye," he said.

"Goodbye, Joseph," the girls chimed in unison.

Joseph was quietly reading in a pub on Charing Cross Road.

Cocteau was an interesting man. He said *The richness of the world was in its wastefulness* and that was a sentiment with which Joseph could agree. He thought of Bukowski. He cared very much for the writings of Bukowski. Bukowski said, *We're all going to die, all of us...what a circus! That alone should make us love each other but it doesn't. We are terrorized and flattened by trivialities. We are eaten up by nothing.*

The man at the bar said, 'Number twenty-six."

Joseph looked up. He was number twenty-six.

The man held aloft a plate and Joseph went to collect it.

"Another drink, mate?" the man asked.

"Can you make a Hemingway?"

"What's in that, then?" the man asked. "I don't really do cocktails, me. Not a cocktails sort of guy."

"I don't know what's in it," Joseph said.

"Can't really help you with that one. Sorry."

"It's alright."

Joseph took the plate and returned to his table. Another man was seated there.

"Sorry guv'nor," the man said, and started to get up. "Didn't realize you were sitting here."

"It's alright," Joseph said. "There's plenty of room for both of us."

The man sat down again.

Joseph looked at his dinner.

"What you got there then?" the man asked.

"Steak and ale pie and gravy and mashed potatoes and some peas."

"Looks good. Food's alright here, you know?"

"Are you hungry?" Joseph asked. "Would you like some?"

"Nah, you're alright, mate," the man said. "Very kind o' you though, I must say."

Joseph smiled. "A lot of people seem to talk about kindness, but very few seem to show it."

"Oh, you are right there, my friend. Nail on the head. Abso-bloody-lutely."

The man extended his hand. "Frank," he said.

"Joseph," Joseph said, and shook Frank's hand.

"Don't let me interrupt your food, Joseph," Frank said.

"You are not interrupting me, Frank."

"So what is it that you do, if I might ask?"

"I read," Joseph said. "I like to watch films sometimes. I meet people. We talk. I discover new things every day."

"But for a job, I mean. What do you do for a living?"

"I used to work for Menella, but then the time came for me to leave and they gave me money and I left. I have been travelling since. I went to France, to Ireland as well. Now I have come here."

"I am a mechanic," Frank said. "I know it's not much of a thing, but I have always loved cars and engines and all that stuff."

"Do anything," Joseph said, "but let it produce joy."

"That's a nice thought," Frank replied.

"Walt Whitman," Joseph said. "He was an American poet. He's dead now, but he wrote a lot of excellent poetry."

"Never been much of a one for poetry," Frank said.

"Poetry is what happens when nothing else can," Joseph replied. "Charles Bukowski."

Frank laughed. "My, you really are an encyclopaedia of other peoples' words, aren't you?"

Joseph paused before splitting the crust of the pie. "Aren't we all? Except that mostly we repeat what we hear without really understanding it."

Frank ruminated. "I think you're right. Fixed opinions. Bigotry. Even racism, I guess."

"That's why people should read more. Read enough opinions and you start to formulate your own."

"You should be the minister for education, my friend," Frank said, laughing. "You should get into politics."

Joseph shook his head. "Being in politics is like being a football coach. You have to be smart enough to understand the game, and dumb enough to think it's important."

Frank laughed out loud.

"Eugene McCarthy."

"Well, Eugene McCarthy better not say something like that around here on a Saturday afternoon. He's likely to get himself a good thumping." Frank laughed again. "Like being a football coach. That is very funny."

Joseph ate some pie. It was good, just as Frank had said.

"So, you lost your job and now you're just travelling around, eh?"

"Yes, I am."

"But you'll have to get another job, I guess."

"I don't know," Joseph said. "It was a dull job and even though I did what was asked of me it didn't really seem to matter that much. That job could have been done by a monkey with a tie."

Frank laughed. "Maybe you should be a comedian."

"Maybe I will just write a book of my own."

"Yes, and then other people can quote you."

Joseph went back to his pie.

Frank leaned forward, rested an elbow on the table, lowered his voice. "Can I ask you a question, Joseph?"

"Of course, Frank."

"Just man-to-man, you know?"

"Yes, please ask me whatever you like."

"I mean, you seem to have your head screwed on right an' everything, and I was thinking only this morning that it would be good to just tell a complete stranger about something that I am running into…just because a problem shared is a problem halved, sort of thing."

"Fire away, Frank," Joseph said. "I'm listening."

"Well, I am not such a young man any more, you know? Not as young as you. And I have this girlfriend, and she's a bit younger than me, and she's never had kids and she really wants kids, and I am not so sure that it would be right for me to take on such a responsibility. I mean, it's a big commitment, not only financially, but also time. It challenges your freedom, I guess is what I'm saying - - "

"Freedom is a responsibility," Joseph said. "Most people do not really want freedom, because freedom involves responsibility, and most people are frightened of responsibility."

Frank raised his eyebrows.

"Sigmund Freud," Joseph said. "But I listened to someone once. They were talking about what it was to have children. They said that having a child was like being given a chance to live your life all over again. They said that living with a child made you see the world the way you saw it when you too were a child. It reminded you of the inherent magic in all things. The world does not change, not really…only the way we see it."

"I get all that," Frank said, "and I've listened to a dozen different people and they say conflicting things, and I really don't know what to think about it now."

"Isn't it the case that you only ask for someone else's opinion to hear them agree with what you've already decided?"

Frank shook his head and sighed. "Maybe, Joseph. Maybe that's true."

"No human relation gives one possession in another. Every two souls are absolutely different. In friendship or in love, the two side-by-side raise hands together to find what one cannot reach alone."

"That is a beautiful thing."

"Kahlil Gibran," Joseph said. He speared a half dozen or more peas with his fork and ate them.

"You are a wise man, Joseph," Frank said.

"Thank you, Frank, but I think we are all wise. I think we become stupid when we start to believe that other peoples' voices are more important than our own."

"Says you, quoting every one and his aunt."

"Voices and words are different, Frank. I read. I try to remember not only those things I agree with, but those I disagree with as well. If we fight what we disagree, we become a victim of our disagreements."

"Gettin' a little bit deep and philosophical for me, my friend," Frank said.

"There have been many wise men and women. No one has a monopoly on wisdom. If someone has said something that is true, why say it differently? That is all."

"Yeah, you got a point there."

"And so, what decision did you make before you asked me?"

Frank picked up his pint glass and leaned back in the chair. "I had decided to become a father...me, at my age. I feel that it would be good to leave someone behind."

Joseph smiled. "Then leave someone behind, Frank."

Frank reached out and gripped Joseph's forearm. "I was drawn here, wasn't I? Do you believe in Fate, Joseph? Do you believe that sometimes we meet the exact person we need to meet at certain points in our lives? Do you believe in that kind of thing?"

"Yes, Frank, I do. I believe in ghosts and *déjà vu* and extra-sensory perception. I believe in magic and the possibility of life on other planets. I believe that Man has everything he needs to solve the ills of Man, and that the earth itself has a cure for all the sickness and maladies from which we suffer. I believe in a lot of things, Frank, but most of all I believe in people."

"Children do that, don't they? They believe in people."

"Yes, they do, Frank. I think we lose the child within ourselves without even noticing, and then we mourn the loss of that child for the rest of our lives."

Frank left.

Joseph finished his meal.

As he returned the plate to the bar and thanked the man, an English art teacher working in Stuttgart posted a *Random Acts of Kindness* logo on-line. Forty-three people shared it within the first minute of its appearance. Underneath the logo it read *celebrate kindness, not celebrity* in small letters.

A girl in Worcester posted a negative comment about it.

Seventy-eight people posted negative comments about her. Nine people unfriended her. One woman even sent her a friend request only to then unfriend her a moment later. She then posted a comment explaining what she had done and why. Fourteen other people said such things as *lol*, *rofl* and *lmao*. The conversation trended on Twitter until someone from Greenwich Village tweeted something about Lady Gaga's hair.

Joseph just left the pub and started walking. He thought he might like to see the National Portrait Gallery, but he was undecided.

16.

The woman from the television company looked a little like Jenny Agutter but her name was Mary Coleridge and she was a liaison manager for a breakfast show that aired every day from six until nine.

Joseph had been called down from his room. He exited the lift and there she was, smiling, her hand extended.

They sat facing one another in deep chairs near the window. To his left Joseph could see out into the street. It had rained again and a petrol spill reflected a whirl of extraordinary colours against the glass.

Mary Coleridge thanked him for seeing her. She thought he looked a little like Johnny Depp, about how he would appear on screen, but she did not say anything. She told Joseph the name of the show for which she worked, and then she said the names of the presenters.

"Yes," he said. "Those names are familiar."

"Well," Mary said, "we were hoping that you might be a guest on the show tomorrow morning."

Joseph frowned. "On the television? Why? Why do you want me to go on the television?"

Mary laughed. She was very pretty. "Because what you are doing is inspirational, Mr. Conrad. This whole movement you have started - - "

"I didn't start anything," Joseph said. "Not that I am aware of."

"Well, whether you intended to or not, the world is beating a path to your door. You have over a quarter of a million people who have liked your Facebook page, and the number of people following you on Twitter is going up by thousands every hour."

"I didn't know I had a Facebook page until someone told me," Joseph said.

"Well, whatever has happened it is exciting, and people want to know about it. It took us two days to track you down, you know? I think we must have called every hotel in London. It's fortunate that you have an unusual name, that's all I can say." She laughed again.

Joseph watched her mouth and her eyes and the way she moved her body. He liked her. She was not hiding from the world like so many people.

"If you want me to come on your television program, I will," Joseph said.

The expression on Mary's face said all that needed saying.

"Oh, that is just wonderful. Just wonderful."

"So where do I go?"

"Well, we wanted to do a piece for about fifteen minutes just after the nine o'clock news, so we could send a car for you tomorrow morning at seven-thirty, if that's okay. That will give us time for make-up and sound and all the usual things."

"Yes," Joseph said. "The usual things."

"You have been on television before?"

"No, I have not."

"Trust me, you'll be fine. I think you will come across very well."

"Thank you."

"So, we just need a little background for our records," Mary said. She took an iPad from her bag and switched it on.

"Joseph Conrad," she said. She typed his name. "So, when and where were you born?"

"Someone asked me about that a few days ago," Joseph said. He smiled and glanced towards the window as a very fat woman walked past in the street. She was eating a pie out of a paper bag, and then she dropped the bag on the pavement. Joseph wanted to ask her who she believed might pick it up for her.

Joseph looked back at Mary. Her fingers were poised over the screen of her iPad.

"Your date of birth," she said.

Joseph smiled and shook his head. "I have not the faintest idea, Mary."

"You don't know your birthday?" she asked.

"Maybe it's on my Facebook page," he suggested.

"Well, if you don't know it, then it couldn't be. I am baffled, Mr. Conrad - - "

"I cannot tell you anything really," he said. "I was born and I don't know who my parents are, and I think I was looked after by some people from a different family, but I can't really get a clear notion of how that happened or why. I remember starting a new job, but I don't recall exactly when it was. I worked for Menella, but I don't work there any more. Before that it's all a bit hazy."

"Did something happen to you?"

"Did something happen?"

"I don't mean to pry, but did you perhaps have an accident or something? Did you perhaps suffer an illness or have a head injury or something? Maybe something happened and you experienced memory loss as a result?"

"Perhaps, yes," Joseph said. "That would explain it, of course."

Mary tapped away on her screen.

"Okay," she said. "And where do you live now?"

Joseph looked around the hotel lobby, and then glanced upwards. "Here," he said.

"Oh," she replied. She tapped on the screen some more.

"It's all very intriguing," she said. She leaned conspiratorially close. "It isn't all a publicity stunt, is it?"

Joseph frowned. "Isn't all what a publicity stunt?"

"This whole thing…I mean, create all this interest, all this mystery, and then we find out it's some sort of street marketing thing for a film or a book or something."

"I don't understand what you mean, Mary," Joseph said, and then he smiled. "Joseph and Mary. Like in the bible."

"Yes, the bible," Mary echoed, and for a split second her eyes manifested concern.

Joseph sat forward in his chair. "I am hungry," he said. "I am going to ask for someone to bring some food to my room."

Mary looked awkward.

"Are you hungry, Mary?"

She hesitated. Then she looked down at her iPad. She cleared her throat. "I don't think it would be such a good idea for me to come and eat in your room, Mr. Conrad."

"If you are hungry you should eat," Joseph said. He rose to his feet.

"I…er…I appreciate the offer, Mr. Conrad, but I think it would be improper…I mean, I am here on a purely professional basis, and…and even though…"

She put the cover on her iPad and pushed it into the bag at her feet. She gathered up the bag, rose from the chair, and stepped away from Joseph. She extended her hand. Joseph took it.

"It was a pleasure to meet you, Mr. Conrad, and a car will be here to collect you tomorrow morning as agreed."

119

"It was a pleasure to meet you too, Mary," Joseph said.

"I hope that you don't take my refusal of your invitation - - " she started. She blushed. "I am sorry," she went on, "but I am very new to this kind of thing, and I really don't feel it would be proper."

"I understand," Joseph said, knowing that he understood nothing at all.

Mary Coleridge backed up, turned away and hurried towards the front of the hotel. Joseph saw her on the pavement, glancing only once at him through the window where he had seen the fat woman with the pie.

Joseph walked to the reception desk.

"How can I help you, sir?"

"I am going on television tomorrow morning," he said, "but now I would like a sandwich."

17

The woman told Joseph to close his eyes and then she sprayed something on his face.

"Good bone structure," she said. "Handsome face. You remind me of Ryan O'Neal."

"I don't know Ryan O'Neal."

"Love Story," the woman said. Her name was Claire. "With Ali McGraw. Such a sad film." She paused for a moment in thought, and then she said, "Keep still," and used the tips of her fingers to blend and smooth whatever she had sprayed on his face.

When Joseph opened his eyes he was a different colour.

Claire put a little lacquer on his hair, and then she took the tissue from around his collar and tossed it into the waste paper bin.

"All done," she said. "Laetitia here will take you to the green room."

The room was not green at all. There was a plate of pastries. Laetitia told Joseph to help himself. He ate two, one of which had custard and almonds, and then his fingers were sticky and he felt a little nauseous.

He sat and waited alone. There were magazines on a table but they seemed to speak of nothing but the trials and tribulations of peoples' personal lives. Such and such a girl used to be fat and now she wasn't, but her boyfriend had left her and she didn't know whether to go on a dancing show. Someone else had tattoos that they regretted. There were several pages of famous people getting out of cars and showing their underwear. Joseph did not know what it meant, and he could not understand why it was sufficiently important to put in a magazine.

Laetitia returned with someone else.

"I'm John," the man said. "Sound technician."

John asked if he could loop a wire through the buttons of Joseph's shirt and clip a small microphone to his collar.

"Of course," Joseph said.

"Just speak normally," John explained. "We can monitor volume from the desk and accommodate accordingly."

"Good," Joseph replied.

"Excellent," Laetitia said. "Then we're all set. Shouldn't be more than a few minutes and I'll come and get you." She smiled. "Have a pastry."

The lights were bright and hot.

Joseph was announced, and he walked behind a partition, and the presenters smiled at him and waited for him to join them on a vast orange sofa.

"Good morning, Joseph," Jane Austen said. "We are absolutely thrilled to have you with us this morning."

Joseph smiled and sat down. Beside him was the other presenter, William Morris, whom everyone referred to as Bill.

"So," Bill said. "You seem to have created quite a stir with your activities."

"Yes indeed," Jane said. "Over half a million Facebook followers, close to two hundred thousand on Twitter, a campaign called Random Acts of Kindness, and people phoning the show to tell us that they met you, that you helped them…even a police officer who said that you had stopped someone from committing suicide."

"I like to help people if I can," Joseph said.

"And what of this occurrence in a hotel in Dublin, Joseph? There is a rumour that you exorcised a ghost from a room there."

"I did not hear any rumours," Joseph said.

"But you did find a ghost there?" Bill asked.

"I am not certain what a ghost is, Bill," Joseph replied. "A human being is spiritual in nature, and sometimes they get lost and you can help them move on. That's all."

"And is this something that happens to you often, Joe?" Jane asked. "You see peoples' spirits and talk to them?"

"No Jane, not often."

"But everywhere you go you seem to create a stir. I mean, you have become a celebrity overnight."

Joseph smiled. His expression was uncomplicated and artless. "I don't understand why there is any fuss, to be honest. I just say what I think, and I try to be helpful, that's all."

"So it seems, Joe," Bill said. He smiled and touched Joseph's arm as if they knew each other well.

"So tell us, Joe…how did all this start?"

"How did what start?"

Jane laughed.

"This project…this movement you've begun," Bill said. "You seem to have caught the imagination of the country - - "

"Not only this country," Jane interjected. "We understand that you were in France as well."

"Yes, I went to France before I went to Ireland."

"And we also understand that you know almost nothing of your own life…that perhaps you suffered an accident and experienced amnesia or memory loss?"

"I don't know anything about that," Joseph said.

"But it's correct to say that you don't know who your parents are?" Jane asked.

"That is correct. I don't know who my parents are."

"And you had a job, but you lost your job?" Bill asked.

"The Human Resources people told me that they were downsizing the company, and they gave me some money to leave."

"Sign of the times," Jane said.

"Yes, indeed," Bill concurred.

Joseph smiled but said nothing.

"So, Joe…tell us how you intend to capitalise on this fever of…of *kindness* that you have instigated," Jane said.

"I don't intend to capitalize on anything, Jane," Joseph replied.

"You are not planning to set up some sort of foundation, perhaps? Help even more people with the money you could raise through charitable ventures?"

Joseph was silent for a moment.

"Everyone is a rest-stop," he said quietly.

John inched up the volume on Joseph's microphone.

Jane leaned forward a little.

"Everyone can be a rest-stop for the defeated, the lost, the lonely, the desperate, the heartbroken. Everyone can offer a warm welcome, a hug, a hot meal, an encouraging word, a shoulder to cry on, a sympathetic ear. We spend so much time telling each other that we are bad or wrong or stupid. That doesn't help. It doesn't make things better. People are lost and frightened enough. They don't need to have it driven home to them again and again. We share our bitterness, resentment, anger, fear and hatred. We promote intolerance and ignorance. We make strangers feel unwanted. People are starved enough for real friendship. Why do we seem so intent on telling our friends about their mistakes?"

Joseph paused.

Neither Jane nor Bill said a word.

"People know when they've made mistakes. People are good most of the time. They try their best. Those with bad intentions make up a tiny minority. Most of the time, even when people do something wrong, they do it because they thought it was a good idea, perhaps because they thought it was their only option."

"So true," Jane murmured.

"People want to feel safe, calm, reassured. They want some space and time to figure out how to deal with their own problems. Give it to them. Let them breathe, especially when they are young. Life can be short, it can be fragile, but it is precious beyond compare."

There was a murmur of agreement in the studio audience.

Joseph looked beyond the bright lights. He had not even realized that there were people out there in the darkness.

"Maybe I am a dreamer," he said. "Maybe I am a fool. Maybe I am naive...but I still believe in the basic goodness of human beings. I still think that being told it's okay, that it might look bad but we can work it out, is better than being told you made a mess of it and nothing can be done."

A ripple of applause came from beyond the bright lights.

"Sssshhhh…" someone said, and the applause stopped.

"I still think that it's better to give people the benefit of the doubt. I think we should err toward forgiveness rather than criticism. What gives us the right to judge others harshly? We all make mistakes, don't we?"

Joseph smiled. He did not know how much he was supposed to say. He guessed he would just go on talking until someone told him to be quiet.

"Pope said to err is human, to forgive, divine. Shakespeare said 'Forgiveness is the fragrance that the violet sheds on the heel that has crushed it.'"

"So beautiful," Jane whispered.

"Forgiveness is not an occasional act, it is a constant attitude," Joseph went on. "Martin Luther King said that, and Confucius said that to be wronged is nothing, unless you continue to remember it."

"Well, you certainly seem to know a lot of quotes from other people," Bill said.

"Other people have said very wise things, Bill. We hear them, we understand them, we even agree with them, but we do not apply them to ourselves or our lives."

More applause from the audience.

"There was a writer called GK Chesterton. He said that to love meant loving the unlovable. To forgive meant pardoning the unpardonable. Faith meant believing the unbelievable. Hope meant hoping when everything seems hopeless."

"And do you believe there is hope, Joseph?" Jane asked. "With all the terrible things that are happening around the world…the terrorism, the violence, the soaring crime rates? Do you think we are nearing the brink of disaster as a society, or do you think we can be rescued?"

"We can always be rescued," Joseph said. "Hope is inexhaustible."

The applause started in earnest then, and it was unheard of from a live television audience on *Breakfast with Bill and Jane*.

"And are you the man to rescue us?" she asked.

Joseph smiled. "No, Jane, I am not here to rescue you. You are here to rescue yourselves." He turned to Bill. "Bill is here to rescue you, too." He looked out beyond the lights to the audience. He extended his hand towards them and smiled with such warmth. "You and you and you and you," he said. "You can rescue not only yourselves but everyone else. Kindness costs nothing. Trust costs nothing. And yet we have convinced ourselves that we should be mean and distrusting. Only we can change that, and that is my hope for the future."

Jane fingertipped away tears.

Bill was speechless.

The audience were on their feet.

By the time Joseph reached the green room once again his Facebook followers had exceeded eight hundred thousand and he was trending number one on Twitter.

18.

People smiled at Joseph as he left the building. They said things like "Great, man," and "Well done...about time we had some truth around here..." and Joseph wondered who had been lying to them.

A security guard called Eric shook his hand and said, "Best go out the back, sir...I think there may be too many people in the street."

Joseph followed him through a maze of narrow corridors and they reached a door that said *Fire Exit – Keep Clear*.

"Take care of yourself, sir," Eric said, and he pushed the bar and opened the door.

Outside there was a crowd of people. They shouted his name – *Joseph! Here, Joseph! Hey, Joseph Conrad!* – as if they knew him, and they reached out their hands and they wanted pictures with him. People clapped him on the back, and Joseph stood amongst them and he didn't understand what was happening.

After a while they went away.

He stood alone in the yard behind the television studio building and it started to rain. He stood quietly and he did not move, and the raindrops fell all around him and he did not get wet.

In a restaurant a woman came and touched his shoulder.

"I am so sorry to disturb you," she said, "but didn't I just see you on TV?"

Joseph turned. He got up from his chair. He did not like to sit when he was addressed by someone standing.

"Yes, perhaps," he said. "I was on the television."

"I cried," the woman said. "What you said was so beautiful...about hope, and trusting one another and being kind. So beautiful."

Joseph smiled but didn't say anything.

The woman waited for him to speak. When she realized he was not going to respond, she said, "I just wanted to tell you that. That was all. It was heartening to hear that on the television."

"Yes," Joseph said. "Good. I am happy you were heartened."

The woman leaned forward suddenly and kissed Joseph on the cheek.

Then she laughed as if she was embarrassed. "I am sorry," she said. "I couldn't stop myself. You are very handsome, you know?"

"Okay," Joseph said.

The woman seemed to be unsure of what to do then.

"I am very happy to have met you," Joseph said, and he held out his hand.

The woman gripped Joseph's hand and shook it.

"Thank...thank you," she said, and then she hurried away as if fearing what she might say or do next.

Joseph sat down again and a girl brought the sandwich he'd ordered.

A man stood over him.

"You are the guy from the TV," he said. "This morning."

"Hello," Joseph said.

"You think all the world's problems can be solved by people being kind to each other," the man said. "You are naïve and stupid."

The man waited for a response.

Joseph had nothing to say.

"There are crazy people everywhere," the man continued. "You see it in the newspapers, on the TV. Murderers, paedophiles, people who will abduct your kids. People get killed all the time. It's in the newspapers and on the TV."

"I don't read the newspapers," Joseph said.

"You don't read the newspapers? How the hell do you expect to be kept informed? What a stupid thing to say."

"Sometimes I watch TV."

"You see the news, right? Terrorists everywhere. The society's finished. The Americans will end up in a war with the Middle East, and then we'll find out that they had those weapons of mass destruction all along. We'll get dragged into it because our own politicians are too weak to say no to the Yanks, and before you know it we'll be in World War Three and we'll all be dead."

"I don't think that's going to happen," Joseph said.

"Then you are naïve and stupid," the man replied, and he walked away.

Joseph watched him go. He paused by the door of the restaurant to say something to someone, and then he looked back and pointed at Joseph.

Joseph smiled.

The man rolled his eyes and shook his head as if exasperated.

Then he left the restaurant and Joseph went back to his sandwich.

When he came to pay the girl at the counter said, "No, it's okay."

Joseph frowned.

"The boss said you didn't have to pay. He saw you on the TV and he said that if there were more people like you in the world then the world would be a much better place and the least he could do was buy you lunch."

"That is very kind," Joseph said. "Thank you."

"You are very welcome, Mr. Conrad."

"What is your name?"

"My name? My name is Rebecca."

"There is a book with your name by Daphne Du Maurier," Joseph said.

"Yes, I know," Rebecca replied. "Last night I dreamed I went to Manderley again."

"Yes, that's it. That's a fine book."

"Good luck," Rebecca said.

"With what?"

"Everything you're doing. Your life, you know? I hope it all works out well."

"Thank you, Rebecca," Joseph said. "That is very kind of you."

Joseph left the restaurant and crossed the street. He needed to buy some new clothes and find a hotel.

The department store had six floors and the men's clothing was on the fourth.

Joseph took one escalator after the other. People he did not know pointed at him. Some took photos with their phones. As he alighted near overcoats and suits, an old man gripped his shoulder and said, "You're that lad off the TV program…the breakfast show."

"I am, yes," Joseph replied.

"Everyone's talking about you," the old man said.

"Everyone?"

"Yes, absolutely. Did you hear about Joseph Conrad, they're saying. That's your name, isn't it?"

"Yes, it is."

"I recognized you. I saw the program. You said some very simple and powerful things. I wish you the best of luck son, but you have to be careful."

"Careful?"

"The truth is dangerous. There are people out there who don't want people telling the truth."

Joseph nodded. "I understand."

The old man shook his head and looked askance at Joseph. "I'm not sure you do, son, I'm not sure you do."

"What is your name?" Joseph asked.

"My name? My name is unimportant."

"Everyone is important. What is your name?"

"My name is Thomas Hardy."

"It is a pleasure to meet you, Mr. Hardy," Joseph said. "And you don't need to be worried for me. I do understand what you mean, and I am not afraid of what might happen."

"Well, I hope nothing is exactly what happens," Thomas Hardy said. "Stick your head above the trench and you're likely to get it shot off."

"I need to buy some clothes," Joseph said. "It was a pleasure, Mr. Hardy."

"Likewise, Joseph," Hardy said, and they shook hands.

The girl who assisted him with his purchases laughed at everything Joseph said, even when it didn't seem appropriate.

He made no attempt to be humorous, but she seemed nervous and excited and her voice was shrill. Her name was Ella, and she had bold auburn hair like Rita Hayworth.

When he was complete with his selection he stood at the till as she swiped his card.

"If you need someone to help you try those on…" she said. She left the sentence hanging in mid-air.

Joseph knew what she meant. He didn't understand why she didn't just say what was on her mind.

"I think I can manage myself," Joseph said, "but I don't think that's what you meant at all, is it?"

The girl blushed.

"You are a really beautiful young woman," Joseph said. "I am a stranger. I was on TV this morning, but that doesn't mean anything. If you would like to have dinner sometime, or maybe go and have a cup of coffee and a conversation, we could find out whether we have anything in common and if we actually like each other."

"Yes," she said. "We could do that. Do you have a mobile number?"

"I don't have a mobile phone, no."

"Okay, do you have Facebook, a Twitter account? I could tweet you."

"I don't have a computer," Joseph replied.

"Oh," she said. "How do I get hold of you? How do you get hold of me?"

"I could come back later when you are finished with your work and we could go somewhere."

"I can't tonight."

"Another time, then," Joseph said, and he picked up his bag.

He knew that Ella was engaged to be married. He knew he would never see her again, and that was exactly how he wished it to be.

Joseph walked less than half a mile and found a hotel. He checked in, again could not say how long he intended to stay. No, he had no suitcase. No, he did not need anyone to carry his bags to his room.

No sooner had he entered the lift than the young man at the desk called the concierge.

"That guy off the TV," he said. "Joseph Conrad...the one that everyone's talking about. He just checked in."

"You sure?"

"As anything." He indicated the computer screen. "See. Joseph Conrad. Room six-o-two."

"Wow," the concierge said. "There has to be a way to take advantage of this."

"That's exactly what I was thinking."

"Get the kitchen to make up a fruit basket, and get some flowers too."

"On it," the young man said.

The concierge picked up the phone and called someone.

19

"What you are saying is not even possible," Herbert Croft said.

He leaned back in his chair. His desk was expansive, a mahogany playing field, and upon it sat curios and mementoes of his thirty years in the newspaper business. To each item was attached a story, and each story was a treasured facet of his life. Here a letter opener presented to him by the 11th Earl of Rutland, a crystal paperweight bequeathed from his first wife's father, a solid silver ashtray purchased at the Grand Bazaar in Istanbul when he was young and impulsive and took a lover. But, in that moment, his attention was upon nothing but Joseph Conrad and the information he was being given by his current affairs editor, Toby Smollett. Toby was the son-in-law of Herbert Croft's cousin, and they enjoyed a first-name familiarity that was unknown to other editors, even the *chief* and *city* with whom Herbert had worked for more than twenty years.

"Here we have a British citizen," Croft continued, "and we know he is a British citizen because he very recently left the country and then returned - - "

"Er, that's where some of the problem lies, Herbert," Toby said.

"What?"

"The passport authorities seem to have lost their records of his exit and entry."

"What?"

"I don't understand. It's all computerized, it's all super-technical, it's a multi-billion pound system, but apparently they have glitches like anyone else. From what I understand, and they are understandably very cagey about telling us anything, they have periodic meltdowns due to the volume of traffic and sometimes there are holes in their records."

"Holes in their records. That's what they said?"

"Yes, but it's unquotable. It's not a reliable source."

"Everyone is a reliable source and everything is quotable, Toby."

Toby didn't respond.

"Okay," Herbert said. "So, what you're saying is that he has no parents, no fixed abode, no wife, no children, no property, no car, no mobile phone. He does not control his own Facebook or Twitter accounts, despite the fact that there are more than a million people follwing him - - "

"More than two million now," Toby interjected, "and that's just on Facebook."

"Whatever," Herbert said, waving his hand dismissively. "The bottom line is that to all intents and purposes he does not exist, except that he has just appeared on the highest-rated breakfast show in the country. Doesn't that seem a trifle odd to you, Toby?"

"A trifle odd, yes," he said.

"We have calls coming in from I don't know how many freelance journalists who need background, and even our own research team, for which I pay the highest salaries imaginable, have been able to find nothing of significance." Herbert paused to catch his breath. He was not prone to irritable monologues and he felt a little lightheaded. "Tell me at least that we have found out who this mysterious Menella is and that we know where he worked."

"No," Toby said, matter-of-factly. "We have not found her, and we have no idea where he worked."

Herbert sat down again. He turned his chair towards the window, towards the vast panoramic sprawl of the city, and he closed his eyes. He breathed deeply for a moment, as if preparing for meditation, and then he said, "He's a ghost."

"I beg your pardon?"

"A spook, a phantom, a sleeper…GCHQ. That's what's going on, Toby. This is some sort of conspiracy."

"I'm sorry, Herbert, I'm not following you."

"Did the television station even vet him before they put him on prime time?"

"They have the kill switch."

"What?"

"They say it's live, but it runs on a five-second delay. That way if someone says something controversial or inappropriate they can cut the transmission before it airs. In truth, almost nothing that's live is actually live. That way they can avoid the time and cost of vetting everyone."

"So, no vetting at all, basically."

"I wouldn't have thought so, no."

Herbert leaned forward and rested his hands on the desk. He looked intently at his cousin's son-in-law. "The only people who have the capability to make someone vanish completely are MI5, MI6, some of these other covert operations units that come under the aegis of national security. Whitehall, that's who's behind it, and if Whitehall is involved then it's political. There's something afoot, Toby, and I want to know what it is."

"You really think this is an orchestrated thing?"

"What else could it be? Think, Toby, think! Someone appears from nowhere. He has no history, no records, no family, nothing. I mean, even this nonsense about the exorcism in the hotel in Ireland. What the hell is that if it isn't some way of protecting themselves? He starts doing something they don't like, he starts going off-program, and they snatch him, say he was crazy, and he disappears."

"I think you're beginning to get a touch fantastic now, Herbert."

Herbert didn't react to the comment. "He becomes an internet sensation, people love him, he goes on television…I mean this *Random Acts of Kindness* movement that seems to be erupting everywhere - - "

"I was on the tube this morning," Toby interjected. "A woman asked me if I wanted to sit down. She said that I looked like I'd had a long day already and it had only just begun."

"What?"

"I know. Shocking. And that's not the worst of it. When I declined, two people acknowledged her kindness."

"You're not serious?"

"I am. Strangers talking to each other on the tube. Smiling as well."

"It's being driven by someone…something…I know it."

"Okay, Devil's Advocate, Herbert. What's the motive here?"

"Oh, Lord only knows, Toby. Politics, finance, it's behind everything. Somebody wants something that someone else has got, or they want to get rid of something they don't want. The Machiavellian lengths these people go to in achieving their own ends you would not believe. I mean, simply take the general political climate right now. Uncertainty, instability, rising inflation, unemployment…whichever way you look at it, we have an unsettled social scene right now. It could be something so simple as giving people something to believe in, something that will rehabilitate hope, distract their attention. However, far more likely as far as I can see, is a much longer program of establishing this Joseph Conrad as *vox populi,* a sort of man of the people, and once he's said a few things and done a few things that have caught peoples' imaginations and demonstrated his credibility, then he can be used to push a political message."

"You really think that?"

"Come on, Toby, don't be naïve. Every political career begins with someone deciding that things need to change and then creating a personality that will facilitate that change. Like Diana said, the country isn't run by those in Commons and Lords, it's run by faceless men in grey suits that haunt the corridors of Whitehall. Politicians are invented, Toby. You really seriously consider that anyone would want to be a politician out of personal choice?"

Toby looked askance at his boss.

Herbert laughed. "I am not crazy, Toby. Okay, it all sounds a little far-fetched, but we have a far-fetched situation on our hands. This Joseph Conrad, whoever the hell he is or isn't, has found himself at the forefront of peoples' minds. He says a few things on television. He comes across very well, very sincere, and what is he selling us? He's selling us the idea that we have stopped caring for one another, that we distrust before we trust, that we should be kinder to one another, that we should look after each other and that there is always hope."

"Sounds really dangerous," Toby said.

Herbert smiled. "For an editor of one of the most widely-read tabloids in the country, you surprise me, Toby."

"How so?"

"You give people a reason to be dissatisfied and they immediately start to wonder how they ended up dissatisfied in the first place. Did you even watch the broadcast?"

"Yes, I did."

"Well, let me recap it for you anyway. That bright and charming young man said that your average man in the street is being told time and again that he is lost and frightened, that the society within which he lives in unsafe, that intolerance and ignorance is promoted, that we spend our time highlighting the mistakes of others, and that we should all be in the business of making other people feel safe, calm and reassured."

"Yes, I got that."

"Okay," Herbert said, his tone indicative of a man who knew he was about to score a point. "Please refresh my memory, Toby. What was our red banner headline this morning?"

"The paedophile ring up north."

"Right. And yesterday?"

"The pop star with AIDS."

"Exactly...and the day before."

"We did the terrorist thing...the extent of active terrorist cells in the UK."

"And the day before?"

"I get it, Herbert."

"Do you?"

"Bad news."

"Precisely. Threats of violence, murder, death, corruption, social dangers, incompetent politicians, the catastrophes that celebrities create in their own lives, and all of it written in such a way as to suggest that it is everywhere and all the time. That is what a newspaper does, Toby. That is the stock-in-trade of the newspaper industry. We are necessarily alarmist in order to save the society from its own complacency and apathy. That is what we do."

"HL Mencken," Toby said.

140

"What about him?"

"The average newspaper has the intelligence of a hillbilly evangelist, the courage of a rat, the information of a high school janitor, the taste of a designer of celluloid vanities and the honour of a police station lawyer. Something like that, as far as I can recall."

Herbert smiled. "Yes, indeed."

"Which begs the question, why are we even involved in this ridiculous business, especially now we are battling with the Great Digital Age and the fact that everyone with a mobile phone considers themselves a freelance photojournalist?"

"Times change, Toby. There's nothing you can do about it, so don't waste your energy fighting it. Right now our job is to keep the readership of this newspaper at the very highest level we can until we find someone to buy this sinking ship. Then we will sell our shareholdings, move to Kent, buy a converted barn and drink ourselves into oblivion. At least, that's what I intend to do."

"And to keep our readership we have to write what they want to read."

"No! Lord almighty, Toby, sometimes you stagger me with your ignorance. We don't print what people want to read...we print what we have decided they want to read. Perhaps in the golden days of the Washington Post it was a case of reporting the news, but not now. The world has moved forward, Toby. Journalism is not longer about *reporting* the news, it's about *creating* the news."

"But I think this time they want to read about Joseph Conrad."

"Yes, but only because someone got there before us. Someone somewhere has decided that Joseph Conrad is the man of the moment.

Someone somewhere has decided that this is what people want to know about."

"William Faulkner."

"Who?"

"The American novelist. He said that the best fiction was far truer than any journalism."

"There's a man after my own heart," Herbert said. "So go write me a Joseph Conrad exclusive, Toby. As long as we use *allegedly* at least three times in every paragraph then we're covered. And if you can't write the truth, then just create some controversy."

Toby paused for a moment at the door. "One other question, Herbert."

Herbert looked up from the paperwork on his desk.

"What if it was a computer glitch at Passport Control? What if there is no agenda here? What if he's just an ordinary, decent guy?"

"Pah! No such thing," Herbert replied, and went back to his papers.

20

Emily Brontë was the first to be identified, and very swiftly the same bright and enthusiastic researcher also connected the dots between her and an American student travelling in France called Charlotte Perkins Gilman.

The researcher's name was Sophie d'Arbouville, and she had joined Toby Smollett's team directly from university.

Sophie found both their postings, the first from Emily which read:

A man called Joseph Conrad just paid for a plane ticket to get me home from Paris. I don't know who he is, but I think he just saved my life.

The second came from Charlotte:

Message for Joseph Conrad. Let me know if you're ever going to swing by again. Would be good to catch up. X

And then Emily again, this time to Charlotte:

Are you in France? Maybe we met the same guy. Contact me.

It seemed that Charlotte had never replied.

Both Emily Brontë and this Charlotte Perkins Gilman were members of the Tiny Ruins Facebook Fan Club. That seemed to be their only visible link. Sophie joined the club, then sent them both a friend request. She received an immediate acceptance from Emily, and sent her a direct message.

Hi. I think I might have met your Joseph Conrad here in London. Can we talk?

Hi, Sophie. I saw him on TV this morning. This is crazy.

Yeah, lol! Amazing, eh?

Yes. So you've met him?

Not really, no. I think I saw him in the hotel where I am staying. I am sure it's him.

He paid for my plane ticket and got me home from France.

I know. Incredible story. I have a friend who works for a newspaper, and he might want to talk to you.

I'm sorry. I'm not talking to anyone right now.

Oh, okay. No big deal. Is everything okay?

Kind of. Well, I am getting some help here at home. I had a few problems while I was away and I'm getting them sorted out.

Okay. Well, I am happy you managed to get home anyway. I don't know much about the way these things work, but my journalist friend might be willing to pay you for any information you have. I mean, I don't know how you're set up and whether or not money is an issue for you.

Ha ha! Money is always an issue for everyone, right?

Yeah, totally.

I am not really able to stay on the computer long. I am away from home. I get limited access. I am getting some help in rehab. I don't think I am the right person to talk to. Joseph did something really kind, and I wouldn't want to say anything about him without his okay. That would seem really wrong, you know?

I don't think anyone has any intention of reporting anything controversial or incorrect.

Lol. This is a newspaper, right?

Yes, of course. But not all journalists are sleazebags.

I am sorry, Sophie. I have to go.

Hang on a minute. Can I just ask you one more question?

No, sorry. I have to go.

"Bollocks," Sophie said as the little green dot disappeared.

The acceptance of her friend request to Charlotte came in two hours later.

Hi. You're the same Charlotte who posted a message about Joseph Conrad, right?

I am, yes. Why, do you know him?

Sophie paused for a moment. She wondered whether she should just be completely upfront with this one.

I am a novice researcher. Just got my first job! I am trying to get some background info on Joseph as he is big, big news here. Are you still in France?

Yes, I am. What's happening there?

You haven't heard?

I am out in the middle of nowhere. Tiny French town. Don't get internet access often. You're lucky to have caught me somewhere where there's a signal.

Oh, wow. This is dynamite stuff. Joseph is on the TV. He's started this whole kindness thing here in the UK.

Kindness thing?

People being kind to each other. It's called Random Acts of Kindness.

That's Joseph?

Yes. Why? Have you heard of it?

It's mad all over Twitter and FB. God, I had no idea that was him!

Yeah, totally amazing right?

Unbelievable. But then kind of not surprising.

Why do you say that?

Because he's an amazing guy.

You know him well?

No, not at all. He just showed up where I was staying and we hung out for one evening. In the morning he was gone.

So you only met him once?

Yes, that's right.

145

So why do you say he was amazing?

Sophie waited for a reply.

None was forthcoming.

The green dot was still there in the chat window.

Charlotte?

Are you going to put what I say in the newspaper?

Not unless you say it's okay.

But I don't really know anything about him.

Okay, no problem. If you tell me something that I think we can use then I will ask you if it's okay to report it. You will have to say it's okay. Right now there's nothing you've said that we would use in a story.

So what are you looking for?

Anything about him, his life, his background. We can't seem to find anything out about him at all.

Have you asked his family?

He has no family.

Lol. Everyone has a family.

Apparently not?

Seriously?

Seriously.

Oh, that is weird.

Yeah, very weird. Okay, so you only met him once. Can you tell me your impression of him? Why did you use the word 'amazing'?

I don't know. There was just something about him. He was really funny. That British humor thing. But I don't know what else. He was just serene. Being around him made you feel serene.

Like calm, right?

More than that. Serene. Like what the word means. It was like hanging out with Gandhi or something! That's probably blasphemy or something. Don't

146

say I said that, but that's what it was like. Whatever it was, I never met anyone like that. Not that made me feel that way.

And you just hung out with him for one night?

Yes, that's right.

Was it an intimate night?

Again, there was no response.

I am sorry. I shouldn't have asked you that.

It's okay.

You don't have to say anything about that.

I'm not going to.

That gave Sophie the answer she wanted.

Okay. Is there anything else you can tell me, Charlotte?

No, I don't think so. Just if you see him, tell him it would be great to see him again and I send all my best wishes for whatever he's doing.

I can do that. Maybe we could speak again sometime.

Sure. Like I said, the internet signal out here is a bit random.

Okay. Enjoy France. Take care of yourself.

Thanks, Sophie. Ciao!

Sophie copied and pasted both conversations into a document and printed them off.

She went off to find Toby Smollett.

21

For a long time, Fergus Hume had known that he was dying. There was no specific medical evidence to support this knowledge, but that did not make him any less certain of it. He believed it would only be a matter of a year or two before he resigned himself to the quiet hereafter. He did not feel any real sense of sadness concerning this; the emotion he experienced when considering his own mortality was one of reconciliation. Why fight the inevitable?

His had been a rare and extraordinary life. The view from his bedroom window gave onto tracts of farmland that he'd bought with his own money and worked with his own hands. He'd raised more buildings than he could ever recall, investing his money in residences, factories, office blocks, cinema complexes and shopping centres. Fergus had worked as if work itself was the singular motivation for life. And here he was, fifty-eight years of age, unmarried, childless, more money than he could ever hope to spend, now consumed by some simple and yet seemingly unanswerable questions: What did it all mean? What had it all been for? What purpose had it served?

However, answers were indeed forthcoming, and from a very unexpected source. Those answers came from the guest of a breakfast television show he'd never heard of, nor ever before seen.

Those answers came from a man called Joseph Conrad.

Fergus Hume made three phone calls and arranged a lunch meeting with three independent financial consultants. He made another call to the hotel he ordinarily used when working in the city, and he drove there himself.

The three consultants – Anthony Trollope, George Meredith and David H. Lawrence – were early. Rare was it that a man summoned by Fergus Hume was late.

"Gentlemen," Hume said. "First and foremost, let me thank you for attending at such short notice. I appreciate that you are all busy, as am I, but I have a number of ideas in my mind and I am a man of decisiveness. If I am seized by a notion, then I often act upon it immediately."

A murmur of acknowledgement circumvented the table.

"As you are no doubt aware, I am a man of considerable wealth. I am also without family and heir. I have, for some time, been considering the possibility of bequeathing my estate to charity, and have already made some provisions for this should I meet a sudden and unfortunate end." Hume smiled, as if here he was enjoying a private joke.

"Having said that, I have the right to change my mind…and I also have the option to start working on humanitarian and philanthropic projects while I am still very much alive and kicking."

A knock at the door, a momentary hiatus in the proceedings as a young woman wheeled in a trolley bearing coffee pots and cups. She served each of the men, and then disappeared.

"And so, I want you three to collaborate together in a research project. And before, you ask a very relevant question – why three of us, and why a collaboration between unrelated financial institutions? – I have learned, from hard-won and somewhat bitter experience that trusting one man with a great deal of money is never a wise idea. Hence, you shall each be responsible to the other two for your collective proposal."

Lawrence raised his hand. "Might I ask what it is that you are considering, sir?"

Hume smiled. "Of course, Mr. Lawrence. I am considering the possibility of establishing a humanitarian and philanthropic foundation based on a comment that I heard on a breakfast television show this morning."

None of the three consultants responded.

"A foundation to promote kindness in all its forms." Hume said. "A foundation that will support, acknowledge, recognize and encourage acts of selflessness, generosity and well-meant kindness."

"And might we ask if this has anything to do with - - " Trollope began.

"A certain Mr. Joseph Conrad?" Hume interjected. "Yes, it does. It most certainly does."

"And would you be considering the possibility of having Mr. Conrad directly involved in this venture, sir?" Meredith asked.

"No, I would not. My business is nothing to do with Mr. Conrad, and I am sure Mr. Conrad has more than enough on his plate to be concerning himself with the likes of me. No, this is a matter for myself and myself alone, though I am sure that individuals will need to be employed for administrative functions, disbursement of funds, further research into philanthropic projects and suchlike. For now, I am merely interested in a realistic appraisal of my net worth. That will include a valuation of assets, an analysis of various properties, shares, bonds, options and trading accounts that would realize further funds if relinquished. Subsequently, we will arrive at a conclusive estimate of how much I could direct towards this without being hijacked and mugged by Her Majesty's Revenue and Customs. Does that make sense, gentlemen?"

"Yes," they all said in unison.

"One further question, sir?" Trollope asked. "Might you have an approximate target of the amount you'd like to release for your foundation?"

Again, a wry smile played across Hume's lips. "Aside from whatever amount I might withhold to maintain some semblance of comfort, I am looking at everything."

"Everything, Mr. Hume?" Meredith asked.

"Yes, Mr. Meredith," Hume replied. "Everything."

Trollope's eyes widened.

Hume leaned forward and looked at the three men in turn. "Let's say something in the region of four hundred million pounds, gentleman. If we could raise that, then we could do some real good around here, don't you think?"

22.

Two hundred miles north, a young woman stepped out of the doorway of a hairdresser into a fierce rainstorm. She backed up immediately, and stood there wondering what the hell she was going to do. Eighty-five pounds she'd spent on her hair, and this evening was her hen night. One minute in such a downpour and she may as well have not bothered. It was absolutely infuriating.

No sooner had she concluded that her only option was to wait it out, than a young man stood in front of her and handed her his umbrella.

"What?" the young woman asked.

"Umbrella," the man said. "For you?"

"But - - "

"Looks like you just had your hair done. Looks great, by the way. Special occasion?"

"My hen night?"

"Wow! Congratulations. That *is* a very special occasion."

The young woman paused. "You're giving me your umbrella?"

"Yes."

"Why on earth would you do that?"

"Because you need it more than me right now."

"That is so kind of you. I don't know what to say."

"You don't need to say anything," he replied, and with that he was gone.

Ward Sister Violet Fane stood at the end of the room and surveyed the beds one after the other. A day did not go by when she did not experience a pang of vicarious guilt and shame on behalf of her patients' relatives. Abandoned. That's the only word that seemed to fit such a situation. These people had been abandoned, their respective sons and daughters awaiting their deaths so houses could be seized, wills executed, estates carved up, money disbursed. It was shameful and shocking and – sadly - a sign of the times.

Violet glanced at her watch. Four minutes to three. For the next two hours, half a dozen old people would glance toward her with that hopeful look in their eyes, that unspoken question on their lips: Any visitor today? No was the answer, and always was the answer. Save for the obligatory birthday and Christmas trips, the awkward thirty minutes, the uncomfortable silences, the glancing at watches, the weak excuses about parking costs, the fact that it might rain, that they need to get Jemima or Stephen or Lilly away to dance classes or Scouts, these oldsters were ignored. It was a sin. There was no other way to describe it.

Violet heard voices in the hallway beyond the swing doors. There seemed to be an inordinate noise out there. Porters flirting with the nurses, no doubt. And nurses who encouraged it despite all her cautionary words.

The noise did not subside. It seemed to be growing.

She scowled, shook her head, turned on her heel and headed down there. Someone was going to get a verbal clattering.

The sight that met Ward Sister Violet Fane's eyes was not at all what she had expected.

Not only was she faced with a horde of relatives she had seen neither hide nor hair of for as long as she could recall, she was also confronted by a rowdy gang of strangers.

One of the nurses hurried towards her.

"All of them are here for visiting hours," she said. "There's even volunteer visitors here from the local church. A teacher has brought half a

153

dozen kids from a school. They have flowers and balloons and chocolates and - - "

"Relatives first," Violet said. "And some of these volunteers can go to another ward. Have the teacher take the kids to the children's ward."

The nurse hesitated.

"Look lively, Nurse Gaskell...we have a lot of patients to cheer up!"

Violet watched Nurse Gaskell corral and herd the visitors. She knew what was happening. This *kindness* business was catching on, and here and there little brushfires were getting out of hand. None too soon, she thought.

She'd seen that young man on the breakfast show. Reminded her a little of Rafe Spall. He'd come across as humble, charming, unassuming. Lovely qualities in a man. Conrad. That was it. Joseph Conrad. God bless him, whoever he was.

There was a quote that always came to mind when Robert Stevenson thought of his post as Shadow Minister for Transport. It came from John Nance Garner, Roosevelt's second-in-command, who said that the 'vice presidency was not worth a bucket of warm spit'. If that was the worth of the vice presidency of the United States of America, then the worth of the UK Shadow Minister for Transport had to be somewhere close to a slug trail. Realistically, there was no hope whatsoever of the current leadership driving the party to an electoral success. Things were not looking good at all on that front. The party, support it though he had – unreservedly, unconditionally – was not in a healthy state. The leadership was weak, the message vague and equivocal, and it had prompted a good deal of soul-searching. If there was nothing to be gained by holding down his current position, if – in truth – he was influencing nothing, changing nothing, then what was the purpose of staying? Would his energy and personal drive not serve some better and more relevant purpose elsewhere?

Robert had discussed it with his wife, Mary.

"You know how I feel, Robert," she'd said. "I feel that a life is wasted unless it is devoted to something you're passionate about."

"I am passionate about politics."

"Of course you are, but politics is an action, not a thought. You have told me what it means...how many times now?"

"Politics is the practice and theory of influencing other people, the making of common decisions for a group of people."

"Right, so there's your answer."

"I am influencing nothing."

"Right."

"So what shall I do?"

Mary smiled. They were in the kitchen. She was unloading the dishwasher, and she paused with a plate in her hand and touched her husband's shoulder affectionately. "Do what you always do, sweetheart. Do what you think is right?"

"I am thinking that I should - - "

"Join that other party."

"Yes."

"Well, we've spoken of it before and you know my viewpoint."

"I do, yes. The greater good."

Mary laughed. "Don't say it like that."

"Like what?"

"Like it's a burden. This other party has some strong ideas, and they're involved in the community. They're not in power, they're not the majority opposition, but they have funding and they're making themselves known. You know, only yesterday one of them showed up here with some fliers and whatever. I don't usually give these guys the time of day. I get enough politics at home, but I listened to him and what they're doing makes a lot of sense. Restoration of community values, looking after one another, not waiting for government to step in. And they also had a few words to say about this Joseph Conrad that everyone's talking about."

"Yes, I've heard."

"What's your take on it? You think it's a stunt?"

Robert shook his head. "I don't know."

"What do your colleagues say?"

"No one knows who he is…or at least that's what they're saying. If it's a stunt, then they've covered their tracks well enough. He seems to have come from nowhere, appears to have no history to speak of. He's certainly an unknown quantity as far as our lot is concerned."

"Well, he is making waves. He may even be the real thing."

"The real thing? I thought that was reserved for Coca-Cola. What is the *real thing*?"

"A force for good, you know? Someone who actually has managed to capture peoples' imaginations, and can effect some kind of change."

"Like Jamie Oliver with school dinners."

Mary swatted at her husband with a dishtowel. "You are such a cynic sometimes."

Robert laughed, grabbed her around the waist and pulled her close.

"I am serious," she said, wrestling free and resuming the dishwasher operation. "Look at what's happening. He shows up, he has a few lines in the paper, a handful of minutes on a breakfast show, and he's got close to four and a half million people following him on Facebook, Lord knows how many tweeting about it, and you can't seem to go anywhere without someone saying the word 'kindness'."

"It's a fad. It's like Bake Off. It'll get everyone excited and then it'll die down."

"I'm not so sure."

"Really?"

"Because it's nostalgic. It's an emotional thing. It makes the older generation think about the war and how everyone worked together for the common good - - "

"Football and war…the only things that gets the Brits pushing in the same direction."

"But for the younger ones there's something else. It's a new idea. It's simple. It doesn't cost anything to be decent to someone else. You know the agenda of the TV and the media. Everyone's different, trust no-one, it's all bad and wrong and getting worse by the minute. I mean, you only have to look at soap operas and whatever. It's crazy stuff. Who lives like that? Tell me a street in England where there's murders and arson and blackmail and kidnap plots and teenagers stabbing their parents on a weekly basis. I think people are getting fed up of it, Robert. I think they've reached a point of saturation. They never really believed it in the first place, and now it's just a stuck record."

"That's just television - - "

"Yes, the soap opera stuff, but I'm just giving that as an example of a broader and deeper problem. We don't live in a society filled with criminals. Not everyone is a paedophile. Read the newspapers and you start thinking that every other person you meet wants to steal your kids, that there's murderers lurking around every corner and in every doorway.

157

That's not the truth. The vast, vast majority of people want to be happy and are interested in other peoples' happiness. I think the truly dangerous elements of our society are a tiny, tiny minority. I really believe that."

"Yes," Robert said. "I would agree with that."

"But the media wants us to believe they're the majority. People aren't stupid, Robert. Government and big business treats us like we're still in kindergarten, but we're not."

"You're going to give me a lecture about political correctness now, aren't you."

"I don't need to, sweetheart. You see right through that the same way I do. I mean, seriously, a bit of sunshine prompts a Class II weather warning. Do they think we're incapable of recognizing when we might feel a bit warm and want a glass of water?"

"So how do we make a difference, then? This Conrad fellow isn't a politician - - "

"Maybe that's the whole point here. Maybe that's what we need. Someone who *isn't* a politician."

"I think that this approach might be just a touch naïve."

Mary paused before speaking. She turned from the sink and looked at her husband. "Maybe so," she said. "But isn't naivete a cousin of innocence? Who was it that said we became adults when we started distrusting people until they gave us a reason to trust? We've lost our trust…in each other, in government, in our own intuition, Robert. The education system is in the toilet, kids are leaving school who not only don't want to read, they *can't* read, and we're taking votes about how many more billions we're going to spend on arms and weapons, all with a view of killing as many people as possible before they kill us."

"You should have been the politician," Robert said.

Mary smiled. "I have too much conscience and too good a memory."

"Says a lot for your choice in husbands."

"You know what? It does, doesn't it? Maybe I should track down this Joseph Conrad and see if he needs a girlfriend."

Robert laughed. "So, what are you suggesting?"

"I don't know many people who can inspire others in an idea the way you can, even when that idea is ridiculous. I have seen you get passionate and enthusiastic about things, and that passion and enthusiasm is contagious. That quality is one of the first things that I fell in love with, Robert."

"And then you found out I was an unbridled sex god as well."

Mary rolled her eyes. "You wish."

"You think I should check this out."

"I think you should keep your options open. Doing something different doesn't mean abandoning your political philosophy and principles. Doing something different just means doing something different."

"I want to make a difference. I feel like I can make a difference."

"Well, all I'm saying is that you could look at why you're not achieving what both of us know you're capable of, and reconsider the directions available to you. Perhaps you could make some calls, see if there's anyone else you could get on board if you started trying to do something effective and purposeful around here."

"The guy has a good message."

"Conrad?"

159

"Yes. It's a simple message, powerful, and it could be supported. It could be translated into something that would really make a difference for people."

"That's the husband I know and love," Mary said. She stepped behind Robert, put her arms around his shoulders and leaned down to kiss him.

"You know what they say about great men, right?" Robert said.

"I do indeed, sweetheart," Mary replied. "Behind every great man is a very surprised woman."

23

MYSTERY MAN OF KINDNESS POSES THREAT TO NATIONAL SECURITY

TOBY SMOLLETT
CURRENT AFFAIRS EDITOR

With a following on social media platforms now exceeding five million, Joseph Conrad is the latest viral internet sensation. There are few who have not heard the name, and yet there seems to be no available information regarding the identity and past of this mysterious man. He's appeared on breakfast television, has featured in numerous magazines and newspapers, and his name has become synonymous with acts of charity, generosity and kindness across the nation. But who is Joseph Conrad, and what is his agenda?

By his own admission, Conrad does not know his own age, and details of his parents seem to be unavailable even to the most astute and dedicated of researchers. Conrad's recent European adventure – where he purportedly aided a young woman from Dorchester by paying her return flight to the UK, and also left money for a French policeman and his wife to aid their house move – has raised questions about the security of our national borders. According to an anonymous source within the Passport Office, records of Conrad's exit and re-entry have been lost due to a 'computer glitch'. That Conrad then achieved some degree of dubious publicity by travelling to Ireland and allegedly 'exorcising' a ghost from the Merrion Hotel provokes a sense of alarm regarding the ease with which the public as a whole accept anyone that presents themselves as a 'celebrity'.

With national security at the forefront of all our minds, and with the ever-increasing need for more stringent controls on social media, the curious case of Joseph Conrad seems both a timely reminder and a needful warning to all of us. Who is Joseph Conrad? Who gave him the right to stand as some kind of self-styled moral judge for our society? The answer to that question is simple: We did. We used our right to freedom of speech and action to elect him to a position of power that exists not in any real world, but in the world of our consciences and hearts. He says we should be kinder. We feel a pang of guilt concerning those to whom we have been unkind. He says that hope is inexhaustible. I would like to hear him say that to the starving millions, the fleeing refugees, those affected by drought, flood, natural disasters and acts of global terrorism.

Conrad preaches his message, telling us that kindness and trust cost nothing, that we have convinced ourselves that we should be mean and distrusting. He goes on to say that we alone can change this, and that this is his hope for the future. Contacting those responsible for vetting and approving individuals who are granted a national audience on our airwaves, our researchers have learned that no such vetting took place. Joseph Conrad - without security clearance, accountable to no one, clearly unwilling to divulge any information regarding his life or history – was given a soapbox on prime-time television. Perhaps we should all take pause for a moment and ask ourselves what we are doing. For all the intense media attention this matter has afforded, very little time has been devoted to establishing the true agenda of Joseph Conrad. We cannot even be sure that this is his name, and yet we are listening to his words, acting on his advice, and following his lead. But where is this unelected leader taking us, and what hidden agenda and ulterior motive lie behind this apparently beneficent façade?

It has been said that the road to Hell is paved with good intentions. Is this the road that we are being directed along by Joseph Conrad? Are we blindly following someone – anyone – who professes to know something of which we are unaware? Are we so naïve and gullible to automatically assume that just because someone says they mean well, they do in fact mean well? Adolf Hitler said he meant well, as did Idi Amin, Saddam Hussein and Osama Bin Laden. Did they not also profess to have the best intentions for their people?

Of course, there will be those who say that such a viewpoint is alarmist. There are always those who challenge our right to be suspicious. However, in times such as these when the killer is always the one we least expected, when the trusted family member, respectable public servant, and – ironically, perhaps – the television celebrity is confirmed as a sexual predator or paedophile, then we might do well to reserve our judgment on those who alert us to the dangers of the seemingly innocent.

Our society functions because of good and decent people, but decency and goodness are all-too-often ascribed to those who have yet to demonstrate such qualities by actions. We only have rumour and hearsay to support Conrad's claims of charity and selflessness. Let us not be fooled into thinking that the giving of money and a few well-chosen words suffice to elevate a man to a position of authority and influence. We – as a nation – give more money to charity than most other countries in the world and we have all shown our willingness to assist, support, advise and counsel those in need of help. Are we all not men and women of kindness? I think we are, and isn't real kindness founded in a practical sense of social responsibility? Alertness should be the watchword in such dangerous and threatening times, and that alertness should now be extended to those who present themselves as saviours or champions. Are we so in need of an internet messiah that we will believe everything we are told without a searching analysis of the facts? Thankfully, it seems, there are more than a few of us who are courageous and independent enough to not be taken in by such a stunt, and I urge our readers to think before they ally themselves to this burgeoning movement that titles itself *Random Acts of Kindness*.

As with all things, the true agenda remains hidden, and this editor – for one – cannot help but wonder if here we are witnessing yet another cleverly-packaged publicity stunt. For what, we do not know, but I am sure it won't be too long before we find out. Then those who have been so effortlessly caught up in the Joseph Conrad 'movement' might be left with a sheepish expression and a sense of profound disappointment.

Caution is the watchword. Trust is something to be earned, not expected.

READERS' COMMENTS

mickdartford

at last, a sensible voice in this middle of this rubbish. this conrad guy is a hoax. people are so stupid.

TaxiMan

Hearing about this guy from almost every fare I pick up. People like the message. What harm is being done? One old guy says it's like the war. Everyone helping everyone else. Old school values.

Baileyclive

Agree with TaxiMan. Newspapers have to see the negative side. Just let the guy do what he's doing. Don't judge people as bad before they've done something to warrant it.

Oxo

Naivete knows no bounds. People are so ignorant and gullible. Voice of reason, anyone? No-one does something for nothing. Everyone has an agenda. Usually it's money. Stop being so easily-led. Sheeple, not people. That's what we've got here.

SaraFina

As a mother of small children, I am amazed that we are listening to this. This Joseph Conrad is everywhere, and no one knows who he is or what he's doing. Everyone knows that the newspapers exaggerate, but this time the exaggeration might be justified. You can't be too careful. That's a cliché because it's true.

JamJarBinks

SaraFina, Oxo, mickdartford. Haters gonna hate. Negative people always look at the negative. Those are the people to ignore. Those are the dangerous ones.

mickdartford

jamjarbinks is the ignoranc one here. stupid name stupid comment. just a idiot.

JamJarBinks

mickdartford is as correct in his viewpoint as he is in his punctuation and spelling.

mickdartford

(Comment removed due to offensive material)

24.

The police did not arrive for close to an hour, and it took a further hour before they managed to clear the foyer of the hotel and the immediate pavement outside.

Still, even as it neared midnight, there were a few on-line news bloggers and tabloid journos hoping for a glimpse of Joseph Conrad.

Joseph himself remained oblivious. He took dinner in his room, sat and watched television for an hour or more, and then he slept.

The very same concierge who had sent flowers and chocolates to Joseph's room let himself in with a passkey around 4.00 am. He removed all of Joseph's clothes, searched them in the privacy of the room across the hall, and then returned them. Cash, a debit card, a passport, a small pencil similar to those found in catalogue stores and a scrap of paper, upon which was written *The Lover - Marguerite Duras*. That was the sum total of the search. Conrad appeared to have no luggage, no laptop, no mobile phone. The absence of the usual was disconcerting. Everything was returned, and then the concierge went back downstairs and called someone from his own mobile.

"Nothing," he said, and then he repeated it to make himself understood.

The next thing he said was, "I know. That makes sense. The whole thing is a scam. How can someone have no laptop, no mobile, no luggage? He's an ex-con, a spook, something. He might be on witness protection. Who the hell knows? Maybe he's just gotten out of a psych place or something. There's something not right about him, that's for sure."

He was quiet for a moment or two, and then said, "Absolutely. Whatever you need. But use this number. Don't phone the hotel, okay?"

The concierge ended the call and put his mobile back in his jacket pocket.

He straightened his waistcoat, took a deep breath, and went back to the front desk.

25

Robert Stevenson waited patiently. His aide – Sam Coleridge – had called ahead, but the hotel staff had been unable to reach Joseph Conrad.

The concierge knew who Robert Stevenson was, and he kept on trying the room.

Eventually, Conrad was found. He had taken his breakfast in the dining room, and before he'd finished eating he'd somehow managed to corral a gaggle of small children who were listening intently to a story he was telling about a man who took his cat to India to meet a tiger.

"Sir?" the concierge said, waving at Joseph over the heads of the gathered children.

Joseph looked up at him.

"Sir, you have a visitor at reception. A parliamentary minister."

"I understand," Joseph said. "I am a little busy at the moment."

"But sir," the concierge continued, "this is a parliamentary minister…the Shadow Minister for Transport, Mr. Robert Stevenson."

"We shall finish the story of the cat and the tiger first, and then we shall talk to the minister." He spoke more to the children than the concierge.

The concierge looked uncomfortable for a moment.

"In fact, tell the minister to come through and sit with us."

"I'm sorry, sir?"

"Tell the minister to come and listen to the end of the story, and then I will speak to him."

"Er…yes, sir…of course, sir."

Moments later the concierge returned, Robert Stevenson and Sam Coleridge in tow.

Joseph Conrad was seated on a chair, the children cross-legged on the floor ahead of him. The parents of the children were still taking breakfast.

"Mr. Conrad?" Coleridge said.

One of the children turned and looked up at these intruding adults. "Ssshhh," he said, which then provoked a few others to do the same.

Stevenson indicated that he and his aide should sit quietly and wait.

"And so," Joseph said, "the cat sat and waited high in the tree for the tiger to come along, and he held the piece of cheese so carefully between his paws, and when the tiger appeared he dropped the cheese and down it went, falling, falling, falling, and it hit the tiger right on the head. Bonk!"

The children laughed as Joseph tried his best to assume the expression of a surprised tiger.

Stevenson looked at Coleridge.

Coleridge frowned, shook his head.

"And so the tiger smelled the cheese, and he wondered where it had come from…but that did not stop him from…"

Joseph paused.

"Eating the cheese!" a little girl shouted.

"That's right!" Joseph said. "And so the tiger ate the cheese."

The story went on. Joseph made faces, different voices, even growled like a tiger when the cat came down the tree and introduced itself. And then the end came, and the man took the cat home from meeting his

Indian cousin, and the cat and the tiger followed one another on Facebook and Skyped every week.

The story over, the children said goodbye to *Mr. Joseph*, and they returned to their parents' tables.

"A fine story," Stevenson said, extending his hand to Joseph, "and you certainly seem to have secured their votes." He glanced back towards the children. "I am Robert Stevenson, and this is my aide, Sam Coleridge."

Joseph stood up and shook Stevenson's hand. He then shook Coleridge's hand and asked them to join him at a table.

"I am going to drink some coffee," Joseph said. "Would you like to drink some coffee too?"

"Yes, that would be good," Stevenson said.

Joseph caught a waiter's attention. "Tom," he said. "Can we have some coffee for everyone?"

"Yes, of course Mr. Conrad."

Tom brought coffee for three.

"That was indeed an excellent story, Mr. Conrad," Stevenson said. "And thank you for inviting us to share it with you."

"It was fun," Joseph said. "The children do not ask how a cat and a tiger can Skype."

"Great imaginations," Stevenson said.

"We all have great imaginations," Joseph replied. "But so often we choose not to use them."

"Yes, indeed," Stevenson replied. So, Mr. Conrad…what is *your* story?"

"My story?"

"Yes…your story. You're all over the internet, you're in newspaper columns, you're on television. Anyone in government would give their eye teeth for this kind of exposure, and yet the message you're communicating seems very basic, very simple, very profound. I guess my question relates more to your intentions than anything else."

"My intentions?"

"Yes…what you're trying to accomplish here, whether or not you have a longer-term strategy in mind, whether you would perhaps consider getting some assistance from within government itself to support you."

"Support me with what, Robert?"

"Your plan."

"What plan?"

"Whatever plan you have in mind now you have the nation's attention."

"Do I have the nation's attention?"

Stevenson laughed, glanced sideways at Coleridge. "I would say so, Mr. Conrad. I would say that you very much have the nation's attention. I get the impression that the country is hanging on your every word much as the children were when you were telling the story."

Joseph smiled. "It was a good story."

"Indeed it was."

"Well, I am not going to say anything differently, no matter how many people are listening."

Stevenson smiled. "So often I hear that statement in government, and so often it is a lie. It is refreshing to hear it from someone who doesn't have a speechwriter."

Joseph paused for a moment, and then said, "I am not sure why you are here, Robert."

"Well, it's very simple, Mr. Conrad. I am the Shadow Transport Minister. You understand what that is, right?"

"I have absolutely no idea, Robert."

"Well, as with any democratic system, there are numerous parties represented in the Commons and the Lords. As you know, we have two predominant political parties, and the party currently in power is our opponent. They have a Transport Minister, and I am his opposite."

"Okay," Joseph replied.

Sam Coleridge watched Conrad closely. He was wondering if Conrad had even the slightest understanding of what he was being told. Either that, or he was exceptionally shrewd and played his cards very close to his chest. Coleridge assumed the latter, for a man with no understanding of the current political scene could never have garnered such media attention. This rise to prominence was being orchestrated and strategised by someone with a great deal of money, and it was merely a question of who and why. He had heard rumour that Fergus Hume was allying himself to this business. Would it not have been more accurate to assume that someone such as Fergus Hume was behind it?

"However..." Stevenson glanced at his aide. "However, Mr. Conrad, it has to be said that perhaps Shadow Minister for Transport is not a position where one feels able to effect perhaps as much change as one would have hoped when one graduated with Honours from Cambridge University." He smiled, but there was an awkwardness in his expression.

Joseph said nothing.

"And thus I am considering my options, and I feel that allying myself to your cause...perhaps, more accurately, allying myself to your message, might be a means by which a more pertinent stand could be made for those things in which I believe."

Stevenson paused and waited for Joseph to respond.

Joseph still had nothing to say.

"I think the point we're driving at, Mr. Conrad," Coleridge interjected, "is that there are many positions in government that possess sufficient authority and influence to effect positive change, and then again, in no way implying that there might be government postings that are, shall we say, somewhat - How shall I put it? - perhaps redundant or impotent. Yes, well...let us just say that there are positions where the *quantity* of change one can effect are perhaps not as great as one might have hoped when one embarked upon one's political journey, for want of a better expression."

Coleridge smiled as if all was crystal clear.

"Yes, exactly," Stevenson said, and smiled too.

"I have no idea what you're saying," Joseph said, "and I don't understand what any of this has to do with me." He looked at Coleridge, then turned and looked at Stevenson. "I don't have anything to do with transport."

Coleridge laughed. Stevenson followed suit. They then looked at one another and shared a knowing glance.

"Let me ask you this, Mr. Conrad," Stevenson said.

"Ask anything you wish, Robert."

"Would you have any issue, either personally or politically, if I chose to pursue the dissemination of your basic ethos, with a view to perhaps expounding on it, bringing it to people in a more digestible form. Obviously, the fundamental sentiment - - "

Joseph looked at Sam Coleridge.

Stevenson stopped talking.

"I have to go now," Joseph said.

Stevenson nodded. "Yes, of course, Mr. Conrad. You must be very busy indeed. I can only imagine the number of things that you have to deal with right now."

"Yes," Joseph said, still utterly bemused by the whole conversation.

"So, in principle, you would have no issue with us piggybacking on your...well, your popularity, Mr. Conrad?" Coleridge asked. "With a view to getting more people to understand and appreciate what you're saying."

Joseph stood up. He looked at the two men seated before him and he said, "I really don't understand why everything has to be complicated. I think people should read more books. I think they should talk to one another and be honest about what they think and what they feel. I think people should try to be kinder and more patient. I think people should take responsibility for what they say and what they do, and when they give their word and make a promise they should do it with their heart, and then try their very best to honour what they said."

"Absolutely," Stevenson said.

"Couldn't agree more," Coleridge added.

"Well, if you want to tell people the same thing, then that's fine by me. The more of us that talk about it, the more people might hear it."

Stevenson smiled. He stood up and extended his hand. "You have no idea how happy I am to gain your approval, Mr. Conrad."

Joseph shook Stevenson's hand, and then Coleridge's. It seemed only polite.

"It was a pleasure to meet you," Joseph said, and then he turned and left the dining room.

Stevenson watched him go, saying nothing.

"What do you make of him, sir?" Coleridge asked.

"I think he is a very canny individual, Sam, a very canny individual indeed. To be honest, I cannot see this as an individual thing. There has to be somebody behind this."

"My thoughts exactly," Coleridge said. "And you heard the rumours about Fergus Hume, I expect."

Stevenson looked momentarily taken aback. Hume was a significant contributor to the other side. "No," he said. "Rumours about what?"

"That he's cashing in, donating a great deal of money to numerous projects, that he might very well be backing this Conrad for some sort of political position."

"Is that so?"

"It's just rumours, sir, but there's rarely smoke without fire."

"Perhaps it might be wise to get an audience with the great Mr. Hume as soon as possible. I would most definitely like to see a financial rug pulled out from under our dear prime minister's feet, eh?"

"Oh yes, sir, that would be exceptional."

"Set it up, Sam. Set up a meeting with Hume. Let's see if there's any substance to what you've heard."

26

That same evening there was a knock on Joseph's door. He had just taken a shower. His hair was wet and he was wearing a robe. He stood by the door and said, "Who is it?"

"It's the floor manager, sir. We have a number of deliveries for you."

"Deliveries of what?"

"Flowers and hampers and other things, sir."

Joseph opened the door and watched as a procession of bellhops ferried in one item after another. There were bouquets, garlands, vases of flowers, hampers from Fortnum & Mason, bottles of champagne and wine, and on and on it went until two tables and half the floor were covered in gifts.

"Why are these here?" he asked the floor manager.

"Because they have been sent to you, sir."

"Who sent them?"

"Er…well, all sorts of people, sir."

"What kind of people?"

"It will say on the gift cards, sir."

Joseph looked at the first card. *With sincere best wishes for all success in your endeavours. Respectfully, the Directors of the Friendship Trust.* Another one read, *A small act of kindness for a man who has inspired kindness in so many others*, and yet gave no signatory.

The cards went on – messages from finance companies, charitable trusts, housing associations, organizations that aided the homeless, even the Police.

The troop of bellhops filed out leaving the floor manager standing there midst the riot of colours and packages.

"I don't understand," Joseph said.

"Don't understand what, sir?"

Joseph held his arms out to indicate the abundance of unexpected generosity.

The floor manager smiled. "I think people like what you are saying, sir."

Joseph frowned. "I don't know what I am saying that is so different or important or special."

"May I proffer an opinion, sir?"

"Of course, yes."

"Well, it seems to me, sir, that people have grown a little weary of all the cynicism and suspicion. Seems that the newspapers and the television have nothing to say but bad news. Did you hear about Toby Smollett?"

"Who is Toby Smollett?"

"He's a journalist. He works for one of the tabloids. He wrote a scathing piece in the newspaper about you."

"About me? Why would he do that?"

The floor manager laughed. "Because he's a hater, Mr. Conrad."

"A hater?"

"Someone who just hates things. Someone who tries to smash anything good. He's a nasty piece of work, believe me."

"But I have never met him. I have never heard of him. Why would he want to write unpleasant things about me?"

"Because that's what we do here, sir. That's what the tabloids do in this country. Anyway, someone spray-painted his car with the word *fascist*, and he's had people protesting outside his house. I think he's gone into hiding somewhere down south."

"Oh," Joseph said.

"I see all sorts come through our doors, you know? Good people, decent people, people who are trying their best to make other people happy with music or books or films or whatever, and then I read something about them in the paper that makes no sense at all. I've even read about things that were supposed to have happened right here in this hotel, and I know they didn't happen."

"That seems very sad."

"It *is* very sad, sir. So I guess that's why..." The floor manager indicated the wealth of gifts. "People are acknowledging you for having the courage to be decent and kind and honest, that's all."

"But most people are decent and kind and honest," Joseph said.

"I know, sir, I know. But I think that a lot of them have been convinced that these are redundant qualities. You've only got to watch two or three episodes of any soap opera and it seems that everyone's an arsonist, a murderer or an adulterer. It's just not true, of course, but people get so caught up in it, you know? You only have to tell someone enough times that they're bad and they start to believe it."

"Yes," Joseph said. "Yes, I can see that."

"So, there we are, sir. These are all someone's way of saying thank you for what you're doing."

"Well, they can't stay here. I am not going to eat all this food by myself. We need to go out and give it to people. The flowers can go to the foyer and maybe in the hallways as well, and I will put all this food in some bags and take it for some of these people I have seen asking for money in the street."

178

The floor manager started laughing. Then he realized that Joseph was not joking.

"Is there someone that could perhaps help me?" Joseph asked.

"Er…yes, sir, of course. Yes, I can have one or two of the bellhops assist you."

"That would be really good of you," Joseph replied.

The floor manager left the room. Within minutes, two of the bellhops that had assisted in the delivery of all the gifts returned. With them they brought sturdy brown paper bags with the hotel logo on the side. They assisted Joseph as he unwrapped boxes of biscuits and cakes, as he collected together all the flowers in one corner of the room, as he separated out fresh fruit and baked goods and pastries.

The three of them left the hotel, and it was mere moments before the journalists and bloggers caught sight of them from the coffee bar across the street.

Minutes later, photos were being posted on facebook and twitter, live feeds were running on the home pages of numerous dailies, and people were getting second-by-second updates on the latest news of Joseph Conrad.

Good Samaritan Donates Food To Homeless

Conrad Keeps On Giving

Joseph's Generosity Knows No Bounds

People started calling the hotel. The floor manager and the concierge went to see the hotel manager.

"People are asking if they can bring things here for distribution," the floor manager explained.

"Things?"

"Food. Clothing. Things for the homeless."

"So we're becoming a distribution centre now?"

"Looks that way," the concierge said, his tone was clearly negative.

The hotel manager smiled. "This is remarkable. This will do wonders for our PR. Yes, absolutely. Have people bring their goods here, and tell them we will do everything within our power to get them distributed to the needy as rapidly as possible."

The floor manager looked at the concierge.

The concierge was evidently displeased. "I'm not sure we'll have enough people to get this under control, sir," he said.

"Solicit volunteers. Tell people they can come and help us. If there are no takers, call the recruitment agency and get as many as you need to make this work. This is good for the hotel, but more importantly it's good for the community."

"But sir - - " the concierge started.

The hotel manager looked up from his paperwork. He raised his eyebrows. "Is there a problem here?"

The concierge was hesitant. He opened his mouth to speak further and then decided against it.

"Good. Then let's get going, shall we?"

The floor manager recruited two bellhops to man the phones. The calls came thick and fast, as did the volunteers. Within three hours, the hotel was sending a constant stream of personnel out into the streets, each of them laden with provisions, clothes and shoes. It wasn't long before other hotels in the neighbourhood got wind of what was happening and decided to get in on the action. The donation program was generating a tremendous amount of social media attention, and they didn't wish to be left out.

More journalists appeared, and as it grew dark Joseph came from the front doors of the hotel and stood on the steps.

Microphones appeared, cameras flashed, questions came thick and fast, and then Joseph raised his hands and everyone fell silent.

The volunteers and the hotel staff continued to bring things out of the hotel.

"What are you all doing here?" Joseph asked the crowd of reporters.

No one spoke.

"Why not do something to help us?" Joseph said. "Don't write about it, just help us. There's a lot of work to do and it's getting dark."

The reporters were unwittingly recruited into the ranks of volunteers. Only a couple of them slunk away.

The work went on unabated all night.

27

The leader of the opposition – William Wordsworth – was informed of the resignation of his Transport Minister as soon as he reached the office.

"What?" he said.

His secretary, Mary Shelley, said, "Yes, sir. He's resigning."

"Why?"

"From what I understand, he's joined forces with Sir Fergus Hume. They've had meetings. He's taking on the job of allocating Hume's funds for all these charitable projects."

"I've heard about this. What the hell is going on?"

"Well, it seems that Sir Fergus has decided to go his own way, sir. He's pulled the plug on contributions to the enemy, and he is setting up his own foundations."

"He's pulled the plug?"

"Yes, sir. So I understand."

"Oh my, that will be a blow over there. And any idea what had prompted this change of direction?"

Mary looked at her boss and wondered if he could have been more out-of-the-loop. For a man who professed to have the good of the British population at the forefront of his mind, he seemed to specialize in knowing very little at all about the British population.

"The Kindness Movement, sir."

"This thing I've been hearing about?"

"Yes, sir. Joseph Conrad. Random Acts of Kindness."

"It's still going on."

"Yes, sir. More than ever. Several of the city's hotels are acting as distribution centres for food and clothing donations for the poor and the homeless. The public are getting behind it like...well, I have to say I've seen nothing like it since Live Aid."

"Hotels? Here in the city?"

"Yes, sir."

"Well, we should be down there pressing flesh and smiling for the cameras, don't you think? Can't we round up a dozen or so junior ministers and aides and secretaries and whatever, get them down there helping out?"

"Yes, sir. Of course, sir."

"Well, let's get on with it, then. I'm amazed that I have to think of these things, Mary. Don't we have an entire staff of PR people or something?"

"Yes, we do."

"Should sack the bloody lot of them."

"Yes, sir."

"I didn't mean that literally, Mary."

"No, sir."

Wordsworth rose from his chair and walked to the window. He looked down into the street. "This thing really has gripped peoples' imaginations, wouldn't you say?"

"I would say so, yes."

Wordsworth turned and looked at Mary for a good ten seconds before speaking. "Why?"

"Why has it gripped peoples' imaginations, sir?"

"Yes, Mary. Why is this happening?"

"Because it's honest, sir. That's what I think."

"Honest?"

"Yes, sir."

"Explain what you mean, Mary."

"Well, this Joseph Conrad...no one seems to know who he is, where he's come from, anything about his past. He just says what he thinks, and he says the same thing to everyone. Doesn't matter if it's a waiter or a newspaper reporter or a TV chat show host, he just says what's on his mind. He's not rude, he's not opinionated, and he comes across as a genuinely good person. He doesn't seem to have any ulterior motive or vested interest. He's not in it for money or influence or trying to get votes. He just seems to be trying to re-establish some basic social values. I think people have grown weary of being told one thing by government and then seeing something else entirely. I think he represents the common man in the way that no politician could ever represent the common man."

"And you believe this? You think he's just an ordinary decent human being?"

"I don't know, sir. All I know is that he's not a politician and he seems to be saying things that people want to hear."

Wordsworth laughed, and there was a cynical edge to his tone. "We all say what people want to hear, Mary. That's the game of politics, wouldn't you say?"

"Okay, then he seems to be following it up with action."

Wordsworth looked unsure of himself for a moment, and then he nodded. "Yes, indeed," he said thoughtfully. "Yes, indeed."

"So I'll get some people rounded up, sir?"

"Yes, yes of course. Anyone who isn't doing something useful right this minute, send them on down there, and then we need to make an appearance. Today, most definitely. I'd like to go out and give some food and whatever to some homeless people. We need to jump on this wagon before it rolls out of Dodge, as they say."

"Yes, sir," Mary replied, and left the office.

Wordsworth returned to his desk and picked up the phone.

"Get me the prime minister," he said, and he waited for just a moment.

"Browning?" he said. "It's Wordsworth. Thought we should meet and talk about all this kindness hullabaloo that seems to be going on."

Wordsworth listened intently.

"Well, absolutely. Couldn't agree more. Yes, I think we're definitely singing off the same hymn sheet this time, Robert."

Wordsworth got to his feet. His expression was troubled though his voice was cheery and affirmative.

"Yes indeed, yes indeed. One hundred percent. Let's say four o'clock then. Looking forward to it."

Wordsworth put the receiver down and shook his head.

"Wretched, wretched man," he said quietly.

He lifted the phone again and called his secretary.

"Mary, I need to be out there doing something pronto. Need to be at Downing Street for four, and I want pictures up on the net before I get there."

28

"It's unsettling, that's what it is," Robert Browning said. He sat behind his Downing Street desk and looked at his political opponent with that same smug self-satisfied expression that he'd assumed since first winning the election. Same school, same house, same rugger squad, same First XI, and yet here they were, the PM and the Leader of the Opposition. When it came down to it, that's all that mattered. Thirty years of personal acquaintance meant very little at all in the political arena, save those very rare occasions when agendas coincided or legislation served both parties.

Perhaps this was indeed one of those rare occasions.

"What it basically communicates," Wordsworth said, "is that the individual counts for something, that the individual can make a difference. Politically that's nonsense of course, but it smacks of something deeper...something, I dare say, conspiratorial."

Browning nodded sagely. "I heard about your Transport Minister. What was his name?"

"Stevenson."

"Yes, Stevenson. Bright fellow, by all accounts. Gone over to Hume, I understand."

"Yes, indeed he has."

"Along with a couple of mine."

"Sorry?"

"I have a couple of defectors myself," Browning said. "Got it in to their heads they could make more of a difference working with Hume on this charity giveaway nonsense he's set up."

"Do you have any details?"

"Very few, as a matter of fact. I have some fellows in internal security working on it, but to all intents and purposes it seems to be exactly what it appears to be. He's withdrawn all support for the established parties. I have no reason to withhold that from you, and I wouldn't be surprised if it's already common knowledge. He's set up some sort of umbrella foundation and is busily ploughing money into humanitarian projects for the community, supposedly."

"Supposedly?" Wordsworth asked.

"It'll be a tax thing, I'm sure. Ostensibly all very philanthropic, but Hume is canny, to say the least. A man like that doesn't just decide to change the habit of a lifetime and give all his money away."

"Unless that's precisely what he's done."

Browning hesitated before speaking, and then he leaned forward. "If that's the truth, then that could set a very dangerous precedent. The political cathedral is less a cathedral and more a house of cards, as we all know. Pull the financial foundations from beneath it, all of which have been grandfathered in for generations, and the whole wretched edifice could come tumbling down on our heads."

"I don't think that's a very likely scenario, Robert," Wordsworth said.

"One thing I've learned in this office, William, is that the unexpected should be expected more frequently than anything else."

"Mmm," Wordsworth ruminated. He looked down at the toes of his shoes. He crossed his legs, uncrossed them again. "The real issue here," he said, "is that we have not the faintest clue who this Conrad fellow is. Unless your people have managed to dig something up."

"The only thing my bright and brilliant intelligence units have managed to find is a woman called Menella Smedley."

"And who might she be?"

"Joseph Conrad's line manager throughout a stint he did at some company in the Midlands."

"Company?"

"Oh, I don't know, some mind-numbing office job. And we didn't so much find her as follow up a call she'd made after that breakfast television appearance he made."

"And what did she have to say for herself?"

"Next to nothing. The man came to her from a recruitment agency which happens to have gone out of business, and he was with her for four years. Did what was asked of him, never caused any trouble, coloured inside the lines, and then took voluntary redundancy along with a few thousand pounds, and that's the point at which all the trouble started."

"He went to France, I understand, and then there was some nonsense about finding a ghost in a hotel in Dublin."

"We've spoken to everyone. Everyone seems to be saying the same thing. He was pleasant, polite, a little eccentric, almost as if there was a screw loose somewhere, but perfectly harmless all the same, and - - " Browning frowned and then smiled.

"What?"

"Seems everyone who was asked for a physical description gave a slightly different description."

"That's not uncommon," Wordsworth said.

"Well, I say a slightly different description...in some cases significantly different, almost to the point where we started to wonder whether there was more than one person going by this name and doing these things."

"Well, if that's the case then the situation is far more serious than we imagined - - "

"However, when shown a photograph of Conrad they all agreed it was the same man."

"Which then presented us with the possibility that he might be some sort of illusionist or hypnotist."

Wordsworth laughed. "That seems a little far-fetched, Robert."

"Have you not seen some of these fellows on television, the remarkable things they seem to be able to do?"

"Well yes, of course I have, but I'm sure it's all staged and prearranged, Robert."

"That very well may be the case, William, but as we speak there is a man by the name of Joseph Conrad who has somehow managed to inspire all sorts of people to do all sorts of odd things."

"We are now labelling kindness as odd, Robert?"

"Out-of-character, then. Now is not the time to be pedantic. We're getting off-track here." Browning stood up and walked to the window. He paused for a second and then turned on Wordsworth. "If Hume sets a precedent and funding starts going in different directions, then we're all in trouble. You know how much Hume has given to this party, and there are more than enough contributors who will follow Hume's lead if Hume starts to make something happen. The fact that we have lost three junior ministers between us in a space of as many days is troubling enough, but if this social media furore keeps going at the same pace the man will have half the country listening to him before we know it."

"He's giving food to the homeless now," Wordsworth said.

"He's what?"

"Apparently he was in receipt of a considerable quantity of gifts, food and suchlike, and he recruited the hotel staff to go out into the streets and give it away. This prompted the other hotels in the area to do the same thing. People got wind of it, started bringing in food and clothing, volunteering to help with the distribution. It's going on as we speak, right here on the streets and in the community centres and what-have-you. Perhaps we could contain it, issue some sort of public disorder - - "

"I don't think we're quite at that stage, William."

"Don't get me wrong, Robert. I think the sentiment itself is all well and good, very noble and all that, but it isn't Christmas and it isn't a coordinated effort like…well, when there's a famine or something. I mean, we get involved in those things because it gives us troops on the ground in different parts of the world without those wretched UN people getting involved. After all, it's been acknowledged for a long time that charitable relief and aid are the subtlest and most effective forms of invasion."

"There are some things even we don't voice, William," Browning said, "even when we're discussing it amongst ourselves."

"So what do you plan to do?" Wordsworth asked.

"As of this moment, very little. No law has been broken, not as far as we can see, and there are no laws against having a facebook page, even if you didn't create it yourself. Then there's the heinous crime of telling people to be kinder to one another, of course." Browning smiled sardonically. "Even getting yourself on television and implying that the press are a propaganda machine for bad news and cultural divisions is not punishable by existing statute. He didn't name names and he didn't say anything that could be construed as libel or slander. What worries us more than anything is that this man appears to have no history. Even his trips out of the country have somehow been lost in our passport system, and it seems that no one has an explanation for that save the usual computer glitch and human error scenarios. It just seems utterly impossible that in this day and age, with all the technology we possess, that an individual can just not exist."

"He does exist. He has a passport. He has a bank account. He did have a job until they made him redundant."

"But nevertheless, with the sheer quantity of computer resources we possess - - "

"Robert, we can't even get the amount of money and the selection buttons on an ATM to line up correctly."

"Yes," Browning said. "Not that I ever use an ATM, but I get the point."

"So, there is nothing to do and there's no way to stop it."

"As we speak, it appears not."

"So we're going to have to let this Conrad fellow keep cheering people up and encouraging them to be kinder to one another."

"It looks that way."

"I don't like it."

"Neither do I, William, neither do I."

"Well, I know you have your best people on it, and the moment he crosses a line we'll have him. Credibility is everything, Robert. Discredit him in some small way, and you will find another thousand ways to discredit him further. As we've demonstrated so many times before, the public can be incited to victimize someone very easily. It's the school bully mentality."

"And the wish to see the crown toppled. In fact, it seems to me that the tabloid machine raises opinions just to see them smashed down again."

"Powerful machine indeed."

"Well, if Mr. Conrad starts to trouble us further, if there are more financial defectors of significance, then a few words in a few ears will soon see some interesting headlines."

Wordsworth nodded in agreement. He rose from his chair and extended his hand. He and the Prime Minister smiled and shook and shared pleasantries.

As the office door closed after Wordsworth, Browning returned to his desk. He shook his head slowly and rolled his eyes. "The man's hopeless," he said to himself. "God help the country if we lose the next election."

Wordsworth, leaving by the front door, glanced back at the building and muttered, "Insufferable bore. God help us all if they get another term in office."

29

The PM's press aide brought through a report detailing William Wordsworth's publicity efforts with the food and clothing hand-out.

His comment upon seeing this, something to the effect of Wordsworth's dealings being as straight as a knotted snake, were heard but elicited no response. A great many things fell on selectively deaf ears in the offices, hallways and landings of Number 10.

Joseph Conrad was utterly unaware that the Leader of the Opposition was using the hand-outs to boost his public opinion ratings. Joseph Conrad was too busy being besieged by Fleet Street and the area managers of numerous charities and humanitarian organizations to concern himself with the fickle business of politics. Amongst those who waited patiently to speak with Joseph was a representative of Sir Fergus Hume's office. His name was Thomas Hood, and he sat quietly in the hotel foyer with a leather portfolio on his knees.

Before working for Hume, Hood had haunted the corridors of Whitehall and the Commons in various guises. His last position of note had been some sort of advisory consultant to the Home Affairs Committee. A more non-specific and untrammelled function would be difficult to find in any government, the general consensus of opinion being that all such *consultants* and *advisors* were lobbyist gangsters, their stock-in-trade nothing less than political leverage, personal blackmail and an ability to sway public opinion through their myriad Machiavellian press contacts. Politics was a dirty enough business as it was, and yet there were always those who were happy to see it dirtier.

In his defense, Thomas Hood has wearied of the public sector and turned to private work in an effort to blanche his soul of former crimes and misdemeanours.   Hume was a businessman through and through, and though Hood had yet to grasp the true nature and import of this most recent sea-change, he felt sure that Hume had something truly grand up his sleeve. If that was not the case, and Hume did in fact intend to give away his entire fortune to charity, then at least the process of doing so would be an interesting adventure.

Hood had been dispatched to speak with Conrad. Hume wanted to get a measure of the man and trusted Hood with that mission. For all his history, connections, personal wealth and influence, Thomas Hood nevertheless found himself waiting in line with everyone else. It was akin to taking a ticket at a supermarket delicatessen counter, and this alone gave Hood a sense of unease. Conrad had to be something other than the rumours suggested. It did not seem real that one man alone could raise such support without possessing some earlier position, credibility or status. LiveAid, after all, had been initiated by well-known and well-loved pop stars; emergency relief actions that engaged the general public routinely followed in the wake of a national or international disaster. But here there had been no such disaster, and Joseph Conrad – again if reports were accurate – was as unknown and unrecognised as a man could be. That, in and of itself, was a marvel in this modern technological age.

At the point when Hood's name was called he had already set himself the task of listening to whatever Conrad had to say, and listening closely. Based on Hood's evaluation of the man, Hume was going to throw a huge sum of money at this *Random Acts of Kindness* movement. Hume was talking millions, perhaps tens of millions, certainly enough to elevate the current operation and activity far beyond anything it could accomplish in its current incarnation. Hume had the power to make this gaggle of disorganized do-gooders into a true force for good in the community, the city, the country as a whole. That was what Hume wished to do, at least ostensibly, and Joseph Conrad was the means by which such a campaign could be more rapidly accomplished.

Hood was shown to Conrad's hotel room by a bellhop, asked if there was anything he required, to which he answered in the negative, and the bellhop left.

Hood stood quietly in the middle of the room. He waited for at least a minute before the bedroom door opened and Joseph Conrad appeared.

The first thing that struck Hood was Joseph Conrad's understated charisma. He wore cotton slacks, an open-necked shirt, a pair of inexpensive shoes. He seemed to look like a million other young men, those types that crowded the train and subway platforms with their earbuds and rucksacks and bedhead hair, every one of them destined to fill a chair in a featureless office and spend their day tapping at keyboards, graphing stock fluctuations or filing insurance claims. Innocuous, unremarkable, one amongst millions. That was how Conrad looked, and he continued looking just that way until he smiled and started to speak. It was then that something else happened, as if the young man was animated by some stronger force.

"Mr. Hood," he said. He walked forward, hand extended. He looked directly at Hood and held his gaze for a good ten seconds.

Hood had unnerving sensation of being looked *through.*

"Please, sit down," Joseph said.

Hood took a seat ahead of the window; Joseph sat on the settee.

"I can imagine how busy your day has been," Hood said.

"Yes, Mr. Hood. Very busy."

"Thank you for seeing me."

"You are very welcome." Again Joseph smiled, and the air around his head seemed to brighten and rarify.

There was no other way to explain it: In Joseph Conrad's presence Hood felt *lighter*, less anxious, most definitely at ease and untroubled.

Was Conrad having pure oxygen piped into the room? Was this all part of the new messiah stunt? It had been done before, would be done again. It was harmless, legal and undetectable. People would leave the room feeling better, and - possessing no identifiable explanation - they would attribute it to the personality.

With Conrad's first question - "So, how can I help you?" - Hood immediately realized that he was late in a long line of visitors, every one of which had arrived with their hands out. Hood's purpose was different: Hood was there not to take, but to give. He therefore set his mind to maintaining the greatest degree of open-mindedness as possible. Bias, prejudice, preconceptions were all swept aside. He wanted to gauge the man as he saw him, based solely on what he did and what he said. The attitudes and opinions of others counted for nothing in that moment, and clarity of perception and observation were all.

"Well, it may very well be the case that I can help you, Mr. Conrad," Hood said. "I come as a representative of Sir Fergus Hume, with whom I am sure you're familiar."

Joseph shook his head. "I do not know anyone called Sir Fergus Hume."

"Oh."

"But no matter, please continue."

"Sir Fergus is a very wealthy and influential businessman, the bulk of his interests being in property and the like, and he is now looking at a number of avenues he might take in order to perhaps - - "

"He wants to do some good with his money," Joseph interjected.

Hood smiled, cleared his throat. "In a nutshell, yes."

"Why?"

"I'm sorry?"

"Why does he want to give his money away, Mr. Hood? Is he guilty and trying to make amends, or is he dying and hopes that he can buy an afterlife?"

Hood laughed, and then realized that Joseph was not laughing.

"I think those are questions that only Sir Fergus could answer for you, Mr. Conrad."

"Then Sir Fergus should have come with you."

"Perhaps yes," Hood replied, "but until you and he have a convenient opportunity to meet, I would like to understand a little of your intention, your overarching mission if you will, so I can best advise Sir Fergus - - "

"You want to go back to Sir Fergus and tell him whether or not I am a fraud, a charlatan, a crook or a thief."

"Perhaps stating it a little bluntly, Mr. Conrad - - "

Joseph smiled. He seemed utterly unflustered. "Shall I tell you what I am, Mr. Hood?"

"Please. Yes, Mr. Conrad. Please tell me."

"I am a human being."

Hood nodded, raised his eyebrows, waited a moment for further and better particulars.

Finally, realizing that this would be the sum total of Joseph's statement, he said, "As we all are, Mr. Conrad."

"I beg to differ."

Hood laughed a little awkwardly. "I'm sorry?"

"As have been most of the people I have talked to today."

"I am not quite sure I understand, Mr. Conrad."

"A human being suggests that the humanity is still extant and functioning, Mr. Hood," Joseph said. "The vast majority of people with whom I have spoken are lost and out-of-touch with whatever it is that makes us human. It is just a simple observation."

"And a very astute one, nevertheless," Hood replied.

"Is Sir Fergus Hume still a human being, Mr. Hood?"

"I believe he is, Mr. Conrad, yes. I think he is an honest, hard-working, decent man who has accumulated a considerable degree of personal wealth as a result of his industry and perseverance."

"Then I shall be happy to meet with him."

"I'm afraid that such a thing might not be possible."

"Then I shall not meet him."

Joseph got up from the settee and extended his hand. "It was a pleasure, Mr. Hood."

Hood looked up, caught off-guard. He was certainly unused to such a forthright and blunt reception.

"I could perhaps call Sir Fergus," Hood said.

"As you wish, Mr. Hood. I know that there are many people who want to speak to me, and I don't know that there are enough hours already."

Hood retrieved his mobile phone from his portfolio.

"Excuse me," he said, and called up the number.

"Yes, Sir Fergus, I am," was the first thing he said.

"Of course, sir," was the second.

"Yes, right here at the hotel. I am with Mr. Conrad as we speak."

Hood paused, listening intently.

"Yes, sir. Of course I have, but he wishes to speak with you personally, sir."

A frown, a moment of unexpected levity as Hood smiled, and then, "Yes, sir. I shall be here."

Hood ended the call. "Sir Fergus will be here in ten minutes, Mr. Conrad…if that's acceptable to you."

Joseph smiled. "Yes," he said. "We have time to order a sandwich. Would you like a sandwich, Mr. Hood?"

"Er…yes, that would be much appreciated. I really am quite hungry."

"I like to eat ham with English mustard," Joseph said, and reached for the telephone.

30

"I am not a man who is used to being deceived," Sir Fergus said. "I don't much care for it, and I won't tolerate it."

Thomas Hood sat quietly in the chair by the window. He had activated the recorder on his mobile phone.

"So, I want to know where I stand with you, young man," Hume continued. "I am not short of a bob or two, and I've paid some smart men a good deal of money to find out anything they can about you, and there doesn't seem to be a great deal to find out. Prior to this job up in the Midlands you appear to have no history, and that doesn't make sense. Now, either there is a huge hole in our national security and social registry system, or you have somehow managed to bleach your past as if it never existed. Which is it?"

Hume leaned back and crossed his legs. He smiled, waiting for a satisfactory explanation.

"I don't know anything about holes, Fergus, and I haven't been bleaching anything," Joseph said.

"Very well," Hume said. "So you tell me what you *do* know."

"Why?"

"Why should you tell me?"

"Yes. Why should I tell you?"

Hume laughed. "Because you've started something important here, Mr. Conrad. Intentionally, or otherwise, you have a nation hanging on your every word. You have politicians defecting. You have discussions taking place in the corridors of Whitehall and behind closed doors. People are interested, intrigued, even worried. Even I, a man of not inconsiderable common sense and intelligence, saw that breakfast show and you gave me pause for thought. You made me think about what I was doing with my time and my energies. That means a great deal."

"If you want to do something good, then you should just do it."

"Of course, yes. Of course I can do something good. But here we have a special opportunity, Mr. Conrad, and if we ally our actions…your support and my funding, then I think we could achieve something extraordinary. I have a lot of money, and I want to know that I am giving it to a man that can be relied upon, a man that can be trusted."

"I don't want any of your money, Fergus."

"No, I understand *you* don't want any of my money, but this organization, this movement you've created…they need the money. Random Acts of Kindness could be a world-changing power for the good. If we get it moving, and moving well, then who knows what we might accomplish. This is something real, something decent and honest, something that stands beyond the influence of politicians and lawmakers and other such criminals."

"I didn't create it," Joseph said. "People have created it themselves, and they can make it happen without me."

Hume frowned and shook his head. "Are you being obtuse for some specific reason, Mr. Conrad, or are you actually a little bit stupid?"

"I think we are all a little bit stupid, don't you, Fergus?"

Hume hesitated, a sense of irritation in his expression, and then he smiled and started laughing too.

"Yes," he said. "I think we have all been very stupid indeed, otherwise how the hell did we end up in this mess, right?"

"Right."

Hood watched the exchange. He didn't understand how, but it seemed that the very canny and very pragmatic Sir Fergus Hume was being charmed by a man who was actually saying nothing very definite at all.

"So, how do you see the future, Mr. Conrad?"

"I imagine it like everyone else, Fergus."

"And what do you imagine for the future...what do you see that can be accomplished with this message of kindness and hope?"

"Maybe that it's possible to restore a desire to be kind, and thus rehabilitate hope for those who feel hopeless."

"Crime, racism, intolerance, bigotry, the dishonesty of the press and the media, the lies and deceptions that are rife throughout business, banking, government...they all fall within our remit if we effect enough change, Mr. Conrad."

"Yes, they do, Fergus."

"It is a big target, Mr. Conrad, and something that could never be accomplished alone. I mean, look at Gandhi, Martin Luther King, Mother Teresa...immense personalities, huge influence, but alone they could not achieve their ends. Only when they had the support of the people could change be made, and you have somehow achieved this. I have seen website forums where people reference your initials and wonder if you are not the Second Coming."

Joseph said nothing.

"And so, simply because I am considering a very substantial investment in something you are connected to, tell me a little of yourself. Prior to this job in the Midlands, where did you live, what were you doing, and where did you come from?"

"I don't remember, Fergus," Joseph said. "I have been asked this question before, by doctors, by people on the television, by journalists, and I cannot tell you what I do not know."

"And that really is the truth?"

"I do not lie."

Hume smiled. "Everyone lies, Mr. Conrad. Even a little white lie is a lie."

"Everyone is not the same, Fergus."

"So, beyond this job - - "

"I remember working for Menella Smedley."

"Yes, we have located her. We spoke to her. She is a somewhat...shall we say *irascible* character."

"She likes to fight."

"Yes, as do so many."

"People who worry about their own importance like to disagree with things, even when there is nothing with which to disagree."

"Oh, you can say that again."

"People who worry about their own importance like to disagree with things, even when there is nothing with which to disagree."

Hume looked momentarily taken aback, and then he was laughing again. "You have a sense of humour, Mr. Conrad. A little dry, a little quirky, but you most definitely have a sense of humour."

Joseph looked at Thomas Hood. Hood smiled politely.

"Have you had any medical tests, Mr. Conrad?"

"For what, Fergus?"

"Perhaps you had an accident, a concussion, a brain injury. Perhaps there may be some physiological explanation for your memory loss."

"There is nothing wrong with me. I have never been ill, and I will never become ill."

"You have never been ill as far as you *know*," Hume said.

"I have never been ill, and I will never become ill," Joseph repeated.

"Very well," Hume said. "As you wish."

"I am what you see, Fergus," Joseph said. "If people wish to categorise, explain, label, investigate, then it is their business. It really is of no concern to me."

"You are not interested in what others think of you, Mr. Conrad?"

"I don't believe I could be less interested, Fergus."

"Well, I must say that that is a very healthy attitude, especially in today's celebrity-driven culture where the minutiae of peoples' everyday business is given a post mortem. Personally, I consider it banal and trite...utterly meaningless, to be honest. These wretched magazines one sees with their alarming headlines and manufactured news stories. Sometimes I am just dumbfounded at the level to which we have stooped as a culture."

"I think someone decided that it was no longer the business of the newspapers to report the news. I think they took it upon themselves to create the news."

"Yes, indeed. Again, a very astute observation."

"Society has lost its way, Fergus. The way is there, but we started to drift, and now we believe there is no way back."

"So, what to do is the question, Mr. Conrad. I propose we establish you as a director of the foundation. We shall call it Random Acts of Kindness. That's the ethos that people have adopted, and there's no reason to change it. We shall endeavour to identify activities and projects that align with that fundamental premise. We shall work industriously in the direction of bettering quality of life through the rehabilitation of both individual and social responsibility. We shall do our utmost to restore some old-fashioned values, a sense of community, a desire to help one another, irrespective of race, colour, creed, religion, gender or sexual orientation. We are all human beings, and thus we are all part of the human race. It has been said that an alien invasion is the only thing that could mobilise and motivate humanity as one peoples, but I disagree. Enough of the backbiting and spitefulness, enough of the racism and intolerance. Enough of this idea that we are all somehow in competition with one another, that the only way you can win is by bringing your fellow man down. It is nonsense. In the last three and a half thousand years there has been a cumulative nine months of peace. Nine months of peace, Mr. Conrad. Since the end of World War Two we have enjoyed three weeks of peace on this wretched planet, and this is the only planet we've got! Where did it all go wrong? That's the question that no one has an answer for. Well, we're not going to even try and answer that question. Far smarter men than any of us have been working on it for as long as records exist and they don't know, so I doubt we're going to come up with anything worth a hill of beans. All we can do is our very best to change what is happening now. We have a chance to do that, slim though it may be, but I would like to die knowing that I somehow made a difference."

Hume looked at Hood. Hood nodded in agreement, even though he did not understand what was actually being agreed here. He had reservations and doubts – many of them – but in that moment he knew that voicing them would not only be distracting, it would be perceived as negative and defeatist by Sir Fergus. He also understood that his initial question had been answered: Sir Fergus Hume really was looking to give away his fortune.

Both Hume and Hood turned to look at Joseph.

Joseph was smiling.

"So…what say you, Mr. Joseph Conrad?"

"I think it is a wonderful idea, Fergus."

"Excellent. Then I shall have my legal team draw up the necessary contracts, agreements, whatever else is needed. It shall be a non-profit organization. It shall have a board of directors, a team of analysts and investigators, the sole purpose of which shall be the identification of worthy causes and humanitarian activities, and we shall do whatever we can to make this country a better place for people. The time has come for change, and we are the men to do it!"

Joseph looked at Hood, his expression implacable.

Hood felt awkward, as if he was once again being looked *through*. Later he would play back the recording of the meeting and confirm for himself that Conrad had neither said nor agreed to anything specific. Sir Fergus had heard what he wanted to hear, even when it had not been voiced.

"It was good to meet you, Mr. Conrad," Hume said, rising from the chair. "I appreciate you're a busy man, and your time is valuable."

Joseph rose too. He and Hume shook hands, and then Joseph shook hands with Thomas Hood as well.

"My people will be in touch," Hume said. "We can reach you here at the hotel?"

"Yes, of course."

"And do you require any assistance on an immediate basis, Mr. Conrad?"

"Assistance?"

Hume smiled, glanced at Hood. "You are unemployed, Mr. Conrad. This is not an inexpensive hotel. I am aware of your bank balance and the money you have been spending. I am sure the foundation can stretch to covering your expenses on an immediate basis. Perhaps, in lieu of any formal dividend assignment, just until we have established the terms and conditions - - "

"I can pay my own way, Fergus," Joseph said. "Your generosity is appreciated, but quite unnecessary."

"Well, at least let me take care of your hotel bill as a personal gesture of kindness, if for no other reason than your having given an old man a renewed sense of purpose."

"As an act of kindness then, yes. That is very good of you, Fergus."

"Think nothing of it, young man," Sir Fergus replied, and he put his hand on Joseph's shoulder.

Pulling his hand back suddenly, he said, "Whoa! That was quite a charge of static!"

Hume grabbed Hood's hand.

Hood recoiled as the same rush of electricity sent a shiver through his entire body.

Hume started laughing, Hood too.

Joseph just stood and waited for them to settle down.

"Nylon in the carpets," Hume said. "Wouldn't expect it in a hotel such a this, but there you go."

"There you go," Joseph said, and opened the door for his guests.

31.

The subsequent announcement of Joseph Conrad's appointment to the Random Acts of Kindness Foundation's board of directors coincided with his twitter following exceeding the three million mark. His facebook followers had long since exceeded that figure twice over, and forums, blogs, online journals and the live feeds of numerous newspapers and periodicals hummed and buzzed with chatter.

Beyond the merely verbal, there was action as well.

Following on from the success of the food and clothing hand-outs, the ranks of numerous Christian charities, Baptist and Methodist ministries, Catholic community outreach programs, and volunteer brigades from a myriad lesser-known denominations were working alongside one another under the umbrella of *Community Kindness*. This loosely-organised but seemingly very efficient collaboration had somehow orchestrated soup kitchens, additional beds and bedding for homeless shelters and housing associations, clothing and footwear drives, hospital visits, meals for the elderly and housebound, projects to remove graffiti, clear common land of rubbish and waste, repair and refurbish municipal and public amenities, and activate non-religious charitable groups into lending their shoulder to the numerous wheels that were turning.

It seemed that everywhere you went something good was being done.

There were a select few who were rankled and aggravated.

A bishop commented that though the projects being undertaken by citizens were all very beneficial, there was a danger in attributing the cause of this to one man. Joseph Conrad was not a saint, after all, and the only real explanation for what was happening was that people were finding Christ's message in their hearts and acting upon it. It was a controversial thing to say, and it was not well-received. A tabloid newspaper ran a sidebar, dug up some unsavoury details about the bishop's personal life, and the church issued a public statement to the effect that the bishop's views were neither those of his congregation nor the church hierarchy. The bishop went to stay with his brother in Devon and was unavailable for comment.

A senior representative of the Police Federation stated that Community Control Orders might need to be issued if the highways and byways became congested with 'armies of do-gooders'. A more senior representative of the same Federation issued a statement to the effect that crime had dramatically fallen, street violence had been almost non-existent for a week, and that the beat officers and PCSOs were ready and able to assist any well-meaning citizen in the execution of any lawful activity that benefited individual members of the public or the community as a whole.

The naysayers and critics were in the minority, and when they uttered their negative comments those comments seemed to fall on deaf ears. The individuals were not openly attacked, they were simply ignored.

One popular and outspoken sports radio pundit seemed to sum up the general mood when he said, "You know what? I'll tell you what I think. People are good. That's the bottom line. That's what's being demonstrated here. People are decent and kind and goodhearted, and it doesn't matter a damn if you're into Jesus or Islam or Jimi Hendrix, people have found an outlet for what is already inside them. Give people a chance to help, and they'll help. This Joseph Conrad guy...what the hell? He's just a guy. He isn't the second coming of Christ or anything else. He's a catalyst. That's what he is. He did some things, he said some things, there's a mystery there because no-one has a clue who he is, and he's caught the attention of the country. From what I've heard this is not now limited to the UK. Stuff like this seems to be going on all over the world.

If people want to knock it down, let them try. Anything good gets attacked. That's just the way it is. Recognise that the people who attack are showing their true colours. Ignore them. Do what you feel is right. Seems to me that the vast majority of people in this world are already onto it, and things are getting better. Good. Does it matter how it started? No. Does it matter who started it? No. Just keep on doing it, and maybe everyone will be a little happier."

People smiled at one another in the street. Strangers initiated conversations on the tube. Politeness became more commonplace. Shop owners and storekeepers noticed a dramatic rise in the number of people returning to the premises because they had been given too much change. A young white man made a racist comment to a bus driver in Hackney. The bus driver refused to move off until the young man apologized. The young man became aggressive and threatening. Eight men, two women and a girl of eight got up from their seats and stared at the man. He became agitated and nervous. He shouted an almost-unintelligible *Okay, sorry! For God's sake, sorry!* and got off the bus. Passengers applauded. Someone had filmed it on their phone and uploaded it to YouTube. It went viral, accumulating over seven million views in less than three hours. The footage was shown on the evening news on seven channels, the young man's face pixilated. Regardless, someone who recognized him posted his name on the net. *Racist Pig* was spray-painted on his front door. His landline and mobile phone numbers were made public and he was bombarded with calls. He disconnected both and left the city.

The hotel where Joseph Conrad was staying had to employ a team of men from a private security firm to man the ramparts. A cordon was erected along the pavement, and journalists formed a vanguard, seemingly interested in photographing and questioning anyone who came and went.

The fact that almost no one possessed any direct or indirect connection to Joseph Conrad seemed unimportant: still they kept asking, almost to the point of harassment. Finally, the manager of the hotel got the police to take action. The journalists and newshounds were herded away, and the road once again returned to normal.

It was three days after Joseph's conversation with Sir Fergus Hume. Joseph took dinner in the hotel restaurant. He drank two glasses of Chablis. He declined dessert but ate a Snickers bar in his room while he watched television. He did not see the news. He did not hear his name mentioned several times on several different channels, and while a mainstream current affairs program devoted close to fourteen minutes to the 'Conrad Phenomenon', Joseph was engrossed in *The Talented Mr. Ripley*. He had never seen the film, and had thoroughly enjoyed it. He especially liked the musical sequence in the club: *Tu vuo' fa' ll'americano, 'mericano, 'mericano...*

A little before midnight he drifted away to sleep. His sleep was untroubled and gentle. His mind was plagued neither by concerns nor unwanted dreams. In essence, his mind was as good as empty, for he did not possess the need to occupy his thoughts with anything but what was right there in front of him. Moments were moments, and once they passed they were redundant. He did not worry, for worry was nothing more nor less than the attempted resolution of a puzzle with omitted pieces. Until he knew, he could not know. If he had given it his attention, he perhaps would have wondered why so many people spent so much time and energy on something so purposeless. The *ifs* and *buts* of life were perhaps useful if a course of action was being considered, but once the course was decided and embarked upon, then the endless wonder about what might have happened had another course been taken was futile.

It said in the Bible, 'Who of you by worrying can add a single hour to his life?' Mark Twain wrote, 'I am an old man and have known a great many troubles, but most of them have never happened.' Even the Dalai Lama commented on the same issue: 'If you have fear of some pain or suffering, you should examine whether you can do anything about it. If you can, there is no need to worry about it; if you cannot do anything, then there is also no need to worry.'

But, most people did not read the Bible or Mark Twain or listen to the Dalai Lama. People listened to the incessant clamour of their own thoughts. Every once in a while they would listen to their friends, and even then it was merely to find agreement for something they had already decided. The world was full of voices, and they were little but noise.

People were riddled with anxieties, and the newspapers and television seemed to do nothing but bolster those anxieties. Every once in a while they would provide a distraction, but the distraction was short-lived and superficial. People talked without communicating; they listened without really hearing; they advised without thinking; they judged without looking; they acted without conscience or responsibility. They did not behave this way because they were stupid or bad; they behaved this way because they lacked an understanding of their own minds and hearts and motivations.

It was easy to be saddened by this, but the sadness would not solve anything. Words were good, but words were only words until they prompted action. Adages and clichés were passed from generation to generation because they carried a grain of truth. Actions did speak louder than words. It was simply a matter of reminding people that they were fundamentally good, each and every one of them, and getting them to act upon that basic goodness.

It was not complicated for Joseph, for Joseph felt no need to agree with anyone but himself. He was not concerned with others' opinions of who he was or who he might be. People had fixed ideas, ulterior motives, preconceptions, misconceptions and so many other things that obscured the truth. They held onto these things in the vain belief that to lose them would be to lose a part of their identity. Identity could not be *lost*. Identity was unique and indivisible. Ironically, it was their efforts to be like everyone else and find agreement in the world that posed the greatest threat of all. Alone, people were rarely bigoted or racist or intolerant of others. That was not the way people really worked.

And so Joseph slept. He knew that soon enough it would all come to an end, at least for himself. He had waited a long time, and now his time had come, and then his time would end.

Perhaps that small detail would prove to be the greatest detail of all.

Perhaps in that way alone, he was just the same as everyone else.

32

The first signs of real trouble followed on the heels of Joseph's meeting with Sir Fergus Hume and the announcement of Joseph's appointment.

Whether or not a number of discreet conversations Thomas Hood had entertained with old contacts in Whitehall and the Treasury were anything to do with this was a matter of speculation. Hood himself had no axe to grind with Joseph Conrad, at least not on a personal basis, but as soon as the full import of Hume's change of direction was understood, the concern in government was that others might follow suit. Hood was an inside line, and everyone had a price. This *Kindness* business was all very well and good, but it was uncontrolled and seemingly uncontrollable. It was a wildfire, and firebreaks were needed.

Perhaps those who sought to control public opinion were anxious about repercussions. The suggestion that individual citizens could make a difference was dangerous, but nowhere near as dangerous as collaborative efforts to effect social change. The public did not understand. They never had and never would. They were little more than children, if truth be known. Politics was complex and expensive. Politicians and bankers and media conglomerates needed to filter information, decide interest rates, enact laws and dictate codes of conduct, and if they did not then the society would tumble into the abyss of anarchy. New ideas were fine, as long as they did not disestablish and unsettle the old and proven ideas that had served to maintain the order of things for more generations than anyone cared to remember. There was a way to do things, and no one had a right to change that way but those who were set to make the most money from it. Everything was dependent upon confidence – confidence in the government, confidence in authority, confidence in the banks and the police and everything else the establishment provided for the good of the people - and that was something that should never be threatened nor undermined.

Yes, there were problems. Every society had its problems. Crime, illiteracy, drugs, violence and corruption were rife, but such issues had been present throughout all Ages of Man. This Age was no different, save that people were informed far more rapidly – and thus influenced far more rapidly – by the internet. The internet served its purpose, of course. It channelled peoples' attention away from the important issues; it overwhelmed them with mindless and banal entertainment; it gave them the idea that they were in communication with one another when they were not really in communication at all; it kept them in their homes and off the streets, and soon they'd be ordering their food, their clothing, their music and films and video games and everything else they required through the web. More than anything, it facilitated a degree of intrusion into the business of their lives as never before.

But, as with all good things, it possessed its liabilities, perhaps more easily demonstrated by current events than anything else. In the absence of social media, no one would have heard of Joseph Conrad, Sir Fergus Hume or *Community Kindness*. The daily diet of generous acts, philanthropy, sharing, giving and helping that now seemed to dominate the airwaves was unprecedented. Newspaper headlines were different. Even the television news – so famously dour and negatively-biased – had taken on a different tone. Ten minutes of bad news, and people started switching it off. Some smart executive suggested a few moments of levity and optimism between stories, and all of a sudden the ratings improved. Ratings were everything. The jovial and slightly tongue-in-cheek dog-on-a-skateboard moment at the end of the ten o'clock presentation had been replaced with a real story about real people doing truly special and extraordinary things. The state channels could be controlled, of course, but the independents could not. At least not so easily. They were utterly reliant on viewer numbers for their advertising revenue, and thus they tailored their transmissions and content to meet a demand. It seemed that the populace was awakening to the idea that it didn't all need to be doom and gloom. Yes, things were tough. Yes, there had been a recession. Yes, jobs were scarce and money was tight and sometimes it seemed that life was nothing but a chain of small catastrophes with few pleasures in between, but was that really the truth? Maybe a change of viewpoint would precipitate a change of reality. Perhaps finding something to like about people was not so hard. The street-life portrayed so vividly and routinely in the daily tidal wave of soap operas – where people lied and cheated and deceived and murdered one another – was fiction. Fiction could be written to order, and the orders were changing.

At least this was how it appeared to be for a number of faceless men in grey suits. Change was not a welcome thing. Stability and predictability were everything. People asking questions was similarly undesirable. People needed to accept the information they were given, and ask no more. Control was not only necessary, it was utterly vital. Anything else was madness and chaos, and that could never be allowed to happen.

More meetings took place. There were hushed conversations in chambers and corridors. Ideas were put forward and summarily dismissed. Media and PR executives were consulted *out of school*, and the summary of all those exchanges was submitted to a man called Richard Dadd. Dadd did not possess an official title, and was unknown to the vast majority of ministers, junior ministers, secretaries and officers of the Crown. Dadd fulfilled a great many significant and consequential roles, none of them permanent, all of them recorded in great detail, and yet the files where such information could be found was privy to perhaps a dozen men in the country. The Prime Minister did not know of his existence, nor did the Leader of the Opposition. The Speaker of the House, the Chief Whip, the entirety of the Commons were all similarly ignorant. There were two or three members of the Lords who knew his face, one of whom knew his real name, and beyond that he ghosted the corridors, listened to what he was told, made his own independent arrangements and executed his orders without question, without variance, without conscience.

And so, the problem of Joseph Conrad finally arrived on Richard Dadd's desk, and the process of damage control was initiated.

Dadd was a man of habit and routine. His background was public school, military academy, officer training, armed forces service, honorable discharge with a handsome pension after more than a quarter century of dedication to Queen and country, and then independent operation. He no longer carried a gun or killed people. He had done more than enough of that to satiate any warrior's appetite. Now he was a very different type of mercenary. He managed a network of confidential informants, insiders, agents and sleepers throughout the United Kingdom and much of the Commonwealth. He gathered information, and he gathered it well. He possessed files on people who were utterly unaware of such files, and within those files were held compromising photographs, recordings of private conversations, snippets of personal matters that could ruin a career, end a marriage, destroy a business. With available technology, phone calls could be intercepted and recorded, text messages and voicemail services hacked, photographs lifted from laptops, desk tops, PDAs and iPads.

Facebook and Twitter could be manipulated, as could Instagram, Flickr, a limitless number of blogs, and any other channel employed for sending, relaying or receiving digital data. Dadd's battlefield was no longer Afghanistan, Kuwait, Iraq or Syria. Dadd's battlefield was literally an *air*field, where the things required to accomplish his mission could be snatched from the ether and held captive.

In the handful of years that Dadd had been providing this very necessary service to the establishment, his loyalty had never wavered. He was – much like the United States Secret Service – allied to an authority, not an identity. The individual and party politics of whomsoever sat in office was irrelevant; it was the office that was served, not the man or woman. In this capacity, and following very precise orders – the majority of those orders dictated by those who held the purse strings behind government – Dadd had orchestrated, planned, strategised and executed projects to both install and topple dictatorships, collapse economies, assassinate heads of state, undermine public confidence in political candidates, expose widespread 'corruption' and thus facilitate takeovers of businesses, industries and manufacturing facilities. Banks and conglomerates had been broken up and scattered to the four winds. Men who had never done worse than absent-mindedly park in a handicapped zone were suddenly on trial for murder, manslaughter, rape, possession of drugs and a catalogue of other offences that saw them ruined, behind bars, even suicidal. Marriages had been ended, personal fortunes destroyed, family estates closed, children denied rightful inheritances, and all from the office of Richard Dadd.

Dadd himself was unmarried. He dressed immaculately, but without ostentation or display. He routinely selected earthy colours – browns and tans and olive greens – much the same as the uniforms he once donned so proudly. He lived alone, dined alone, his apartment situated on the upper floor of a Georgian townhouse near Belsize Park. He did not maintain a car, did not own a television nor a stereo system. Visiting him, had ever such a thing been possible, you would have found a suite of rooms not so different from a million unremarkable hotel suites across the world. Dadd was a perfectionist. A place for everything and everything in its place. He did not have a cleaner; he did not need one. He did not need a cook; he routinely ate out, and on the odd occasion when he ate at home he was more than capable of preparing an adequate breakfast or late supper. He lived alone and maintained a perpetually clean kitchen. This, according to Bukowski, pretty much guaranteed him possessive of the most detestable spiritual qualities. Dadd did not drink, nor did he smoke. He did not enjoy the use of any recreational drug. He slept well, did not snore, never got sick, and had you been asked to estimate his age you would have placed him a good ten years younger than his actual age of fifty-five.

As for family connections, there were none. Dadd was an only child, had been orphaned at seven, raised thenceforth in institutions, and was of a truly institutional mind.

His life, outwardly, was remarkably quiet and sedate. Those who occupied the same building knew him as Mr. Dadd. No one was sure of his forename. He was polite, exceptionally well-groomed, evidently of independent wealth, never seemed to entertain any guests, never made a sound, and possessed the capacity to occupy the lift in such a way as to go completely unnoticed. That faculty did not only apply to his home turf. Dadd was invisible everywhere. People continued conversations within earshot, and every single word was received, registered, remembered.

Routinely, people were unaware that he'd been present, and thus were more than surprised when their private moments became public.

Dadd was an enigma, a paradox, a puppetmaster, a kingmaker, a spy, a charlatan, a thief and a liar. He possessed no conscience, no remorse, no regret.

Within hours of his assignment to the Conrad problem, Dadd had recorded every known sighting and incident involving the man. He'd obtained the names and immediate familial and personal details of Menella Smedley and several work colleagues from the same company. He knew the property that Conrad had occupied for the period he'd worked in the Midlands. He knew the names of Conrad's neighbours. He located the name of the hotel where Conrad had stayed in Paris, though any official record of his departure from the UK and arrival in France seemed to be missing. Dadd located the name and address of a young woman from Dorchester for whom Conrad had bought a plane ticket home using his debit card at a travel agency. The young woman was called Emily Brontë, and she had flown into London and been collected by her father. From Paris it seemed that Conrad had taken a train to Montlucon, and here spent some time with an American student called Charlotte Perkins Gilman. This was surmised from comments on Facebook and another social media forum. Again, specifics regarding his travel seemed unclear. Conrad subsequently appeared in Toulouse, and here was involved in some sort of incident. Details were uncertain, but Conrad was questioned by the gendarmerie and then released. Conrad's next appearance was in St.-Gaudens near the Pyrenees, and here he had given a not insubstantial amount of money to a couple by the names of Alphonse de Lamartine and Madeleine de La Fayette.

From France, Conrad had flown to Dublin. For this trip Dadd located the first official record of an airport arrival and security processing. Conrad had taken a room at the Merrion, and was quick to feature in several on-line blogs and forum entries relating to spiritualism and suchlike. According to one Charles Maturin, a supposed historian and medium, Conrad had exorcised a ghost from a room at the Merrion. Maturin noted in one blog entry that he had called the hotel, spoken briefly with Conrad with a view to meeting the man, and yet had found him 'unwilling to converse on the matter, guarded, surprisingly nonchalant about his own gift, of very unclear motive'. Dadd smiled at this comment. What else could be expected when crazy people talked to crazy people?

Next was London, and here Conrad stayed in Covent Garden. By this time there was a rapidly-increasing social media following with the attendant irrelevances, inconsistencies, uncertainties and idiocies. A second incident with the police was recorded. Apparently Conrad had encouraged a suicide not to throw himself under a train and had wound up in an interrogation room for his trouble. Dadd lifted the interview notes out of the police computer system but they were unspecific and meaningless. There were a few comments from a police psychologist called Samuel Johnson. According to Conrad himself, he'd never been interviewed by a mental health professional nor admitted to a psychiatric facility. Johnson – it appeared – had advised that Conrad be detained under some provision of the Mental Health Act, but a couple of reporters had shown up and derailed that plan. Conrad was subsequently interviewed by a Police Public Relations Coordinator called Isabella Banks. She noted that Conrad had no disagreement or upset with the way in which he had been handled, and had no intention of filing any suit against the police for wrongful detention. Conrad was apologetically released without charge or caution.

Conrad then started to appear in the press, and that led to the breakfast television appearance.

Dadd watched a recording of the television show. He listened to what Conrad said, studied his body language, employed his many years of experience in the business of interrogation, and yet could not clearly identify what he was seeing. The man was a contradiction. He appeared backward, almost as if he suffered from some form of autism or Asperger's Syndrome, and yet his mannerisms did not fit.

Dadd drew no conclusion. He did not need to draw a conclusion. He had a specific mission target to accomplish, and personal opinions were of no consequence or concern.

After Conrad's television appearance, the social media interest became a storm, then a tornado. A *Random Acts of Kindness* concept was promoted, a logo designed and made available free-of-charge. Tee shirts were printed up, and people posted endless selfies as they engaged and participated in these supposedly charitable and humanitarian endeavours.

Qui bono? was the question that occupied Dadd's mind. Who was benefiting? Where was the money in all of this? Was this a publicity stunt for something as yet unknown? It seemed doubtful, taking into consideration the fact that Conrad himself had not directly encouraged anyone to do anything. But then, maybe that was the point. Maybe that was the real genius behind this, for there was no doubt in Dadd's mind that this had been created by someone of great intellect and wit. But still, the question nagged: *Qui bono?*

Toby Smollett, a Fleet Street sleazebag of epic stature, railed against the Conrad movement in his current affairs column, but it seemed to provoke nothing but a tirade of abuse against Smollett himself. Smollett had written the article as Conrad's star was rising. Bad timing. The key was waiting until the star was in decline, and then the proverbial boot could go in to assist that decline. The public were sheep. They followed one another mindlessly. On one hand they forever supported the underdog, on the other they loved to see the mighty fall on their asses. The tabloids worked on this premise almost exclusively. Appeal to their innate jealousy of others' success, they could muster a fury of unjustified hatred with one cleverly-worded headline. Dadd knew all too well how such media outlets could be manipulated, for he had orchestrated such things countless times himself.

All that remained was Sir Fergus Hume, Shadow Transport Minister Stevenson, a couple of defectors from the House, and a handful of vocal junior ministers and secretaries who were bright enough to recognize the publicity advantage of allying themselves to Conrad's message without actually doing anything to support it. Hearsay had it that there were other political financiers looking to divert funds, to collaborate with Hume, to start making waves in government, hence Dadd's assignation to the case. The entire thing needed to be reined in. As had been the case with so many earlier instances of public support for philanthropic and charitable activities, it was simply a matter of removing the power of the identity, in this case Joseph Conrad. Keep the spirit of the thing alive, but take away the personality. Don't deny the unwashed masses the idea that they were doing something independent, free-thinking and beneficial, but ensure it was only an idea. The officially-acknowledged and recognized government representatives were to be afforded credit for everything, come what may. Ascribing credit to outsiders, free agents, unknown parties and those who were not on the *payroll* was a carte blanche invitation to trouble and disorder.

Having studied and tabulated everything available, Dadd made some calls. He gave specific instructions to three journalists, assigned a retired Metropolitan detective superintendent the task of fleshing out Conrad's family background, personal history, employment record, financial affairs, connections, friends, associates and acquaintances, and then called a man he had not spoken to for several years.

"No one is clean," Dadd said. "Everyone is dirty. Everyone has their laundry. Find it for me. Paedophile, sex offender, petty thief, porn addict, ex-junkie...I don't care what it is, it's there. I'm calling you because no one else has dug deep enough. Someone is behind this character, and that someone may have paid to bleach Conrad's history. I need to know who did that, why, and what they've hidden. Usual rate, plus a ten percent bonus if you come back to me within forty-eight hours."

The call ended.

Dadd rose from the table in his living room and entered the kitchen. He switched on the kettle, took a cup from the tree mug, a decaffeinated Earl Grey teabag from a small earthenware container on the countertop, and he waited for the water to boil.

He felt the expected frisson of excitement.

He tasted blood on his teeth.

The hunt was on.

33

A major editorial feature across the centre pages of the largest-circulation Sunday supplement provoked a significant increase in social media activity. Between Facebook and Twitter, Joseph Conrad's collected entourage now exceeded fifteen and a half million people.

Dadd read the article. It told him nothing he did not already know. It was more padding and supposition than anything else. However, it affirmed the *idea*, and that was not helpful. He was not unduly discouraged. Gandhi had nice ideas, as did Martin Luther King, Mother Teresa and Nelson Mandela. No matter, they all died, and the strength of their ideas died with them. That was just the way of the world.

Sowing the odd comment here and there through different online forums to begin the process of discrediting Conrad was clumsy, unreliable and easily traced. The likelihood of discrediting Conrad with one awful crime was also impractical. The real issue was the lack of history. It made no sense at all that Conrad possessed no records. In this day and age it was preposterous that someone could sit beneath the radar for that long and go utterly unrecorded. No, there was some other factor here, and that factor was so basic and so fundamental – perhaps so unlikely – that everyone had missed it.

Conrad had appeared, as if by magic, but magic did not exist. Conrad had come from somewhere. This was where Dadd's attention needed to be focused, and in this instance he really felt the need to look into it personally. Delegation was a vital skill, and Dadd had no difficulty employing a considerable team of people, all of whom possessed their own areas of expertise and experience. For some reason this was different. This was something he wished to do for himself, perhaps just to prove that he was a step ahead of the police, the television, newspaper researchers, and anyone else who may have had an interest in this individual.

Logic and reason clearly dictated that a man could not exist within a first world twenty-first century society and not leave his fingerprints everywhere. Possess a computer or iPad, mobile phone, a GPS and a credit card and you could always be found. The system had been created in such a way as to inhibit everyday routine activities without leaving a trace. It was indeed a matrix, and passage through that matrix was impossible without intricately-positioned tripwires being triggered. If you bought a sandwich, a cup of coffee, if you sent a text, answered an e-mail, made a visit to the supermarket, employed any one of the multitude of internet search engines to check an address, log onto google maps, order a pizza or check your bank statements, then you were located. You could not hide. That was how it was supposed to be. It was necessary for national security, for defence of the realm, for social and political stability. Perhaps the uninformed and unwashed, those who spouted forth about violations of privacy and human rights considered it evil, but it was a necessary evil. Their resistance was borne out of ignorance, and there had to be certain individuals within a society – individuals such as himself – who could shoulder the burden of responsibility.

Dadd went through Conrad's television appearance frame by frame until he found a clear and defined image of the man's face. He processed the image through facial recognition software and verified that all twelve key features were specific and precise. He uploaded the image and it's map and initiated the sequence that would compare that map to every face recorded on every CCTV camera in the country. Images from streets, offices, police stations, train platforms, public transport, doctors' waiting rooms, shopping centres, hospitals, schools, university campuses –

everywhere and anywhere a CCTV camera existed, irrespective of whether or not it had been placed there by a city council, a company, a shop owner or a private citizen – could be compared to Joseph Conrad. Dadd took a month-long section that began a fortnight prior and ended a fortnight after Conrad's first appearance. There would be billions of images. It could take weeks, but then again it could take fifteen minutes. Dadd just had to let it run and see if Conrad appeared.

34

Joseph Conrad had been watching TV all morning. The things he had seen had puzzled him. There were shows that seemed to be nothing more than people shouting at one another. They hurled endless accusations of infidelity, deceit and conspiracy against people they had once loved, especially people to whom they were related. Everyone spoke at the same time, even the show's host. Nothing was resolved and people resorted to crying and fighting. The host seemed to encourage this, and security men had to physically remove guests from the stage.

Another show featured a judge who made decisions concerning unpaid loans, stolen property, incidents of unfaithfulness and domestic abuse. People pleaded their cases. She listened dispassionately, often interrupting them to tell them what she thought, even when her viewpoint was evidently biased or unsubstantiated. Her word was law, however, and both plaintiff and defendant had to comply with whatever ruling she meted out.

Yet another show concerned the trials and tribulations of young women trying to find wedding dresses. Weddings were important, of course, but the stress and drama that seemed attendant to identifying a dress seemed both disproportionate and manufactured. People became hysterical. One girl sobbed so much that she couldn't breathe and they had to turn off the camera.

On it went, channel after channel of bad news, melodrama, over-inflated scenarios and argumentative family members. After an hour, Joseph felt dizzy. He felt he would perhaps go mad if he listened to any more.

Standing quietly before the window, he wondered what had happened to the people of this city, this country, this planet. They had lost their way so very subtly, so very easily, and it had happened without them ever really understanding what was going on. Intolerance, racism, bigotry, infidelity and murder had become commonplace, paraded on the nightly news, on the covers of magazines, spoon-fed every day of the week through soap operas and chat shows. It was like a silent, slow-motion tidal wave, and it found its way into every crevice, every crack, through every gap and hole. It had become so prevalent and pervasive that people just accepted it as normal. This was the way life was; there was nothing that could be done; keep your head down, don't make trouble, look after number one.

This was not the way Joseph remembered it.

This was not the way it was meant to be.

He knew he did not have long, and he did not know if there would be anyone following in his footsteps. He had made a difference, but it was slight and transient, and if he was not here to continue the work then it could all come undone in a heartbeat.

He closed his eyes and breathed deeply.

He could feel the heart beating in the chest, the blood through the veins, the pulse in the temple, the quiet sense of resolve in his mind.

There were no memories save the brief moments he had shared with his neighbours, those he had met on his travels, the people from the newspapers, the radio, the television.

There were so many good people, but they had been blinded by so many distractions and diversions. Importances had been relegated to the status of irrelevance. Priorities had become meaningless. Time had collapsed in such a way that only those things that were happening *now,*

now, now were of any significance. There was no long-term view, no concept of consequences and repercussions, and all the while the sky grew darker, the horizon ever more distant, the chance of reversal less and less likely.

Nothing was ever lost, nothing and no one ever beyond redemption. Of this, Joseph was certain. It was merely a matter of perseverance until the very last breath, and then – if nothing else – he could say he'd done his best.

That was all that had been asked of him. In truth, that was all that had ever been asked of anyone, but they had been misled into thinking that not only was their best not good enough, it was actually futile.

Perhaps the greatest lie of all was that no one human being could make a difference.

Joseph turned from the window. He knew he would have to speak. He knew a statement was overdue and inevitable. Perhaps tomorrow, the next day. It would be simple enough to arrange. Everyone wanted to talk to him. Everyone believed that he had something of value to say.

So be it. He would accede to their demands.

He would give them a statement, and then see what happened.

Joseph left the room and headed down to the lobby. Reporters appeared as if summoned. Joseph simply smiled and waited for the clamour to stop.

There was silence then, as if everyone present was holding their breath, and Joseph smiled.

"Tomorrow," he said. "Noon. I shall answer all questions with a statement. I am happy to do it here, though I believe that may upset the running of the hotel...so if someone wishes to choose a location and arrange some transportation, I will speak there."

With that, Joseph smiled once again and turned to walk away.

The clamour of questions erupted once again, louder than ever.

Joseph stopped, turned back, said, "Noon tomorrow," and then he made his way back up the stairs without another word.

35

At four a.m., Dadd was woken by a signal from his mobile phone. Already he had seen numerous images of Joseph Conrad at various locations in London. Hotel foyers, the airport, several city centre streets, handing out food and clothing to homeless people.

The footage that now appeared on his phone was something else entirely.

It was dated four weeks and four days prior. It showed Joseph Conrad in a hospital corridor. He was dressed in an open-backed robe. He stood in a corridor, almost motionless, and then he turned and walked away from the camera.

Dadd quickly identified the hospital and calculated the distance. He could be there within two and a half hours, traffic permitting.

Dadd showered and dressed. He uploaded the footage from his phone onto a DVD and made a second copy for good measure.

He was on the road within thirty minutes of receiving the notification. Joseph Conrad had been in hospital. That much he knew. There was no question in his mind that this was the same individual. This was something that no one else had found. Of this he was sure. This was a lead, something tangible and concrete, something that might very well answer the question that Conrad himself seemed unable to answer. Hospitalisation suggested injury, perhaps brain damage, perhaps amnesia. Conrad was certainly odd from a behavioural perspective, and this revelation might solve not only the question of his origin and history, but also serve to undermine all the credibility and importance with which he'd been invested. Prove he was nothing more nor less than a brain-damaged, delusional misfit and the entire problem of Joseph Conrad would disappear for ever.

Dadd smiled inside. He knew he was on to something.

The traffic was minimal. A slow on a small section of the motorway lost him little more than a quarter of an hour. He called ahead, instructed the receptionist who took the call to inform the hospital administrator that he was on the way and required an appointment. When Dadd was told that the administrator's diary was fully booked, Dadd explained where he was coming from and why. He did not tell the truth, but gave the approved response when doors needed to open and people needed to get out of the way.

Dadd arrived to find the administrator – a Miss Clara Balfour – waiting for him.

"I'm sorry if there was some confusion," she started, "but it seems that whatever memo or e-mail was sent to alert us about your visit - - "

"There was no e-mail," Dadd said.

For a moment, Clara Balfour seemed unsettled, and then she and her visitor reached the door to her office. She opened it, indicated that Dadd should step inside.

"Can I get you something…a cup of tea, some water perhaps?" she asked.

"Tea," Dadd said. "Moderate strength, no milk, no sugar."

"Yes, of course," she said, and put a call through to her assistant.

Dadd leaned forward and placed a DVD on the desk in front of Clara.

Clara looked at the DVD, then up at Dadd. She knew before he even opened his mouth that it was bad news.

"On this DVD is a section of footage from one of your own CCTV cameras," Dadd said. He paused as Clara's assistant came through with the tea. The cup and saucer were placed carefully on the desk ahead of Dadd. He thanked the girl, allowed her to leave the room, and then took several small sips of the tea in complete silence before setting the cup down again and addressing Clara.

"This patient was under your care on the date specified on the footage. I need to know his name, the reason for admission, the treatment administered, the address given, the date of discharge, and any other information you have on file."

"I am sorry, Mr. Dadd, but - - "

Dadd smiled like a reptile. Clara was momentarily reminded of Randall Boggs in Monsters Inc.

"You understand where I am from, Ms. Balfour."

"Yes, of course I do, Mr. Dadd, and believe me, we are always willing to extend any and all courtesies, but such information is confidential - - "

"Ms. Balfour," Dadd interjected. "I have a mobile phone in my pocket. On it you would find the personal numbers for the Minister for Health, the Chief Hospitals Administrator, the Director of Public Safety, the Hospital Services Ombudsman…and I could go on and on. Every official body that is directly or indirectly concerned with your management of this hospital can be contacted within a moment, my dear. I understand your concern for confidentiality and security, but I am the very personification of confidentiality and security." He reached for his tea and took another sip. He set the cup down once again and leaned back in the chair. He hitched his trousers and crossed his legs. "Now, you have a choice. It is a simple choice. You find me the information I have requested or you find another job." Dadd smiled patiently. "Do we understand one another, Ms. Balfour?"

Clara Balfour felt the colour drain from her face. Her heart was beating a little more rapidly. She really didn't like this man, and she didn't doubt for a moment that he did in fact possess all those telephone numbers, and that he would make calls, and she would find herself in a most unbearable situation.

"Do we have nothing but what's on the DVD?" she asked.

"You have just a face to go, Ms. Balfour. You need to determine where this footage was taken, which camera, which corridor, which unit. You need to go back through your records and find every member of hospital staff that was working during that period of time and show them this face. You need to find out who he is. Everything beyond that will be very straightforward."

"You understand that I have over seven hundred staff and locums and temp nurses, and this may have been nothing but an A&E visit - - "

Dadd didn't say a word. He reached for his tea, took another sip.

"Good tea," he said quietly, and smiled.

"I'll get onto it immediately," Clara said, and rose from her chair.

Dadd rose too, took a card from his pocket upon which was printed his name, a telephone number, and nothing else.

"I will take a room at a nearby hotel," Dadd said. "Please do not call with progress reports or reasons why it can't be done. I need a name. I need dates and times. Nothing more nor less than that."

"Yes, Mr. Dadd," Clara said, and she opened the door for her visitor.

Dadd left the room and headed down the corridor. He did not ask to be shown the way out, and Clara did not offer. Richard Dadd seemed

235

like the last person in the world who would either require or ask for assistance with anything.

It was simple enough to find Menella Smedley.

Dadd called her from the car before leaving the hospital car park.

"He worked for me for four years," she said. "Quiet guy, conscientious. I don't really know what to make of all of this."

"Four years, you say?" Dadd asked. "And you hired him?"

"Yes, I did."

"And why was he made redundant?"

"Downsizing. No other reason. I mean, aside from the fact that he became quite odd, there was nothing about his work that would have prompted a dismissal. It was simply a company thing. Nothing personal."

"He became quite odd," Dadd repeated.

Menella laughed nervously. "I mean...well, I don't know what to tell you, Mr. Dadd. I don't want to say *challenged*, but that was how it appeared. He would look at me like I wasn't there. He would say things that seemed calculated to irritate me, but I don't think that was his intention at all. It was only after he'd gone that I actually realised how...well, how *calm* he seemed to make the place."

Dadd closed his eyes. Dealing with ignorant people was exhausting.

"Okay, Miss Smedley, give me the specific time period of Mr. Conrad's employment."

She did so.

"And how long before his departure did this change of attitude occur?"

"Well, only a little while, I would say."

236

"How long is a little while, Miss Smedley?"

"Just a few weeks, I guess. Three or four weeks, maybe."

"Is that as specific as you can be?"

"Yes, it really is. I'm sorry. It was a gradual thing. I didn't see him every day anyway, but as we started looking at downsizing I was in the office more frequently, and I had a more direct and regular contact with all the employees in that division."

"But, as far as you can recall, the change in Mr. Conrad's attitude became apparent no more than four and no less than two weeks prior to his taking redundancy and leaving the company."

"Yes, that's right. I would say that was accurate."

It was not accurate at all, but Dadd said nothing.

"Okay, Miss Smedley. That's very helpful. If I need anything else, I will call you."

"Is he okay?"

"Sorry?"

"Is Joseph okay? I mean, I know he's been in the paper and on the TV and everything, and I know all this fuss is being made about him, but…well, I just wondered whether he was okay himself, you know?"

"I am quite sure he is perfectly well, Miss Smedley," Dadd said. "I must go now. Thank you for your help."

With that Dadd ended the call and started the car.

Two hours before Joseph was due to make his statement, Richard Dadd received a phone call.

He'd taken a room at a nearby hotel, had enjoyed a pleasant dinner and a surprisingly restful night's sleep. He did not doubt that Clara Balfour would move heaven and earth to find her mystery patient.

Someone would recognize this 'Joseph Conrad' and the web would start to unravel.

Dadd was not himself prone to flights of fancy or imaginative wanderings, but he had pondered the possibilities of this case. His conclusion, as yet to be confirmed or disproved, was that Joseph Conrad had been admitted to hospital following some sort of accident or injury. He suspected a head trauma, a resultant case of amnesia, a serious omission in hospital security on the part of Ms. Clara Balfour, and a man on the street with no memory, no bearings, no past and no home. Ultimately, there would be nothing mysterious about it. Joseph Conrad was neither special nor different. Human beings were human beings. There was no such thing as magic. Everything had an explanation, even when no explanation seemed possible. Ignorant people wanted to believe that there was something greater than what they saw and heard with their own eyes and ears. That's why they were ignorant, and that's why they would remain ignorant.

And so, a little while after breakfast, the expected call came. Dadd was in his room surveying the day's headlines on his laptop.

"We have a name," Clara Balfour said.

"Yes," Dadd replied.

"The man in the footage was admitted under the name Joseph Conrad," Clara said.

"I shall be with you shortly," Dadd replied, and he ended the call.

36

The venue selected was the grand ballroom of an old city hotel. The hotel had not asked for payment for the room. The publicity value alone was priceless. It seemed the entire press corps was present, the turn-out comparable to that of a royal wedding or first-born.

Joseph had been collected from the hotel where he'd been staying. The reception area was crammed with people. Cameras flashed. People shouted questions. The noise was deafening. A pair of hotel security guards had elbowed their way through the crowd and Joseph was being escorted out behind reception, down a long corridor which led into what appeared to be a laundry room. From there they went through another door, yet another, and Joseph could see the kitchen through a series of porthole windows in the corridor. At the end of the corridor was a fire door, and through this was an external yard. Here a car waited for him. The driver exited, opened the door, and indicated for Joseph to get inside. Joseph did so.

The car was moving even before the door was closed, and he held onto the armrest as the driver passed through a narrow tunnel and swerved into the road. The number of reporters and photographers outside the hotel was several times that of those inside, and those flashguns kept popping even when the only picture they were likely to get was the back end of a rapidly disappearing car.

"Madness," the driver said.

"What is?" Joseph asked.

"The paparazzi. The things they'll do to get a picture of a celebrity. It gets worse and worse as time goes on. Barmy if you ask me…utterly barmy. Don't know why it's so important. Don't know why they can't just leave people alone, let them get on with their own lives."

"Celebrity is the chastisement of merit and the punishment of talent," Joseph said, and then added, "Emily Dickinson."

"Build you up to smash you down again," the driver said. "I've heard some stories, let me tell you. Fame is a drug, you know? People get hooked. It can lead to tragedy."

Joseph smiled. "Everything can lead to tragedy," he said. "Even the greatest happiness can lead to tragedy. It's called being human."

"You know the writer J.G. Ballard?" the driver asked.

"I know of him, yes."

"He spoke about the banalisation of celebrity."

"A kind of banalisation of celebrity has occurred: we are now offered an instant, ready-to-mix fame as nutritious as packet soup."

"That's it," the driver said. "That's it exactly. You know that off-by-heart. That's amazing."

"I read a lot of books."

"So do I, Mr. Conrad, so do I. Only thing that keeps me sane."

"You should carry on reading books," Joseph said. "Books are the quietest and most constant of friends; they are the most accessible and wisest of counsellors, and the most patient of teachers. Charles William Eliot."

The driver laughed. "Never trust anyone who has not brought a book with them. Lemony Snicket."

"You don't have to burn books to destroy a culture. Just get people to stop reading them. Ray Bradbury."

"Let us read, and let us dance: these two amusements will never do any harm to the world. Voltaire."

"People can lose their lives in libraries. They ought to be warned. Saul Bellow."

The driver started laughing. The hotel was up ahead and he pulled over to the side of the road.

"I so very rarely meet anyone who loves books as much as me," he said. "You can imagine how much waiting time I have in this job. The other drivers, they moan and complain about it. I love it. Gives me so much time to read."

The driver reached over and opened the glove compartment. It was jammed with books.

"You should look in the boot," he said. "I must have three or four dozen in there. I leave them there for a while until I know which ones I am going to read again. The rest of them I donate to charity or I take up to the hospital library."

"This is a good thing," Joseph said.

"Your hotel's up there, sir...but I think you can see that."

Joseph leaned left and looked up the road. A crowd of people thronged the entranceway.

"I shall go," Joseph said. He reached his hand out and said, "It was a pleasure to meet you."

The driver took his hand and they shook.

"What is your name?" Joseph asked.

"Algie Blackwood," the driver said. "Algnernon, officially, but everyone calls me Algie."

"An honour and a pleasure," Joseph said.

"Hopefully we'll cross paths again, Mr. Conrad," Algie said.

Joseph smiled, and there was a hint of sadness in his eyes.

He climbed out of the car and started up towards the waiting crowd.

37

Dadd arrived at the hospital and was greeted by Clara Balfour.

"We located a nurse and an orderly who remembered your patient," she said. "He was an A&E walk-in on the day of the footage."

"And he was admitted as Joseph Conrad."

"Yes, he was."

"And the date?"

"Here," Clara said, and indicated the manila folder on her desk.

Dadd scanned the enclosed report. There was almost no information, but what information there was served to support his theory. Conrad's admission to the hospital took place just four weeks prior to leaving his job. The receiving nurse had reported bruising, grazing, a head trauma, other minor injuries consistent with a fall. The fact that Conrad had asked about a bicycle several times suggested that he had been involved in a collision of some sort. That was supposition, but suppositions were useful. He had a day, a timeframe, a geographical area, and even though there had to be several hundred CCTV cameras to capture such incidents, he could call upon several hundred people to sift through that footage and find what he was looking for.

"So," Dadd said, "it seems that Mr. Conrad was admitted and examined by an A&E nurse…but there seems to be no indication of further consultation by a doctor, no x-rays, no treatment…" He let the statement hang in the air.

Clara Balfour shifted uncomfortably in her chair. "No, Mr. Dadd."

"He left the hospital."

"It appears that way, yes."

"He got up and walked out of the hospital."

"Yes," Clara said nervously.

Dadd closed the file and nodded his head slowly. "Not good," he said, relishing the unease in the atmosphere.

"No," Clara said. "Not good."

"And there was no internal follow-up to find out where this patient had mysteriously vanished to?"

"No, Mr. Dadd, there wasn't."

"And how many instances of this kind of thing would I be likely to find if I had an admission and discharge audit done in this hospital?"

Clara was silent for a moment. She had never felt so awkward and inept in her life. "Too many, Mr. Dadd."

"Yes, Miss Balfour," Dadd said. "Too many."

He smiled like Randall Boggs and slid the manila folder towards Clara.

"I would like to tell you that this is not important," he said. "I would like to tell you that this incident is of no great significance, but that would be a lie...and I do not lie, Miss Balfour. The simple truth is that a patient was admitted and examined. He was then permitted to walk out of the building without being stopped by medical staff, by orderlies, by receptionists or security. Not only that, but there has been no official inquiry into what happened. The admission report is there in black and white, is it not?"

"Yes, it is," Clara said.

"And yet there is no doctor's report, no discharge report...nothing."

Clara nodded. "That is correct."

Dadd took a moment to inspect the fingernails on his right hand. He could sense the woman's agitation and mental disturbance. It was like standing near a firework, uncertain if it had been lit. There was a quiet thrill inherent in such moments, and they were to be savoured.

"What to do?" he finally asked. "What indeed?"

Clara Balfour opened her mouth to speak, but Dadd raised his hand and silenced her.

"Is not a question for you to answer, my dear," he said. "As of this moment, it is the very least of my priorities."

Dadd rose from the chair and buttoned his jacket. "We'll speak again, Miss Balfour," he said, and then he left the room.

Back in his hotel room, Dadd called the Home Office. He asked for an extension, waited to be connected, and then said, "It's Dadd. I'm going to give you a location, a time frame and a five-mile radius." He then explained very carefully what he was looking for, and impressed upon his contact that speed and confidentiality were of utmost importance.

"I need to know as soon as you find anything that could be relevant," he said. "Do not wait for a second. Call me on this number and e-mail the footage to the usual secure box."

Dadd ended the call. He ordered tea from room service and switched on the television.

Much to his dismay, the very first channel he viewed was running a report on the arrival of Joseph Conrad in the foyer of a city hotel.

The pavement outside the front entrance was crowded with reporters and onlookers.

Conrad himself seemed effortlessly calm and untroubled.

Dadd wasn't so much irritated as resigned. How many times he'd pressed for further restrictions and limitations on press freedom he couldn't even recall. He'd never been one to withhold his opinions on the matter, and there were many in office who concurred. The press was a tool of government. The press dictated public opinion. It did not pander to the whims and fancies of an uncertain and superficially-minded populace. The media was a propaganda machine, and people could so very easily be swayed. Discussions and debates about freedom of speech and freedom of opinion were just so much noise and nonsense. People were incapable of thinking because they did not understand the world. The truth was powerful, and people needed to be protected from it.

Dadd's tea arrived. He sat once again and watched as Joseph Conrad was escorted to a table at the head of a grand ballroom.

Conrad sat down, in front of him a forest of microphones, a bottle of water, a glass.

Conrad smiled.

"I am not who you think I am," he said. "I don't know who you imagine me to be, but I am just the same as everyone else. You have questions, and I think I may disappoint you with the answers I give, but I am happy to give you those answers."

Conrad paused for a moment.

The atmosphere was electric.

"So…what is it that you want to know?"

38.

It became very obvious very quickly that a hundred reporters asking a hundred simultaneous questions was never going to work.

Joseph got up from the chair. He looked directly ahead. He didn't say a word. He just stood there with a quiet smile on his face and waited for the room to settle.

Once order was restored he sat down again. "Perhaps I could just talk for a little while," he said. "Seems the world is so full of noise that no one has a chance to be heard any more. And then, perhaps, when I don't have anything left to say, we could go through the room and see what questions still remain. Maybe that would be simpler."

There seemed to be no disagreement to Joseph's proposal.

"People keep asking me who I am," he started. "Who are you, where do you come from, why do you have no history? People seem to be intrigued and unsettled when they cannot identify you and put you in a box. I am asked if I have an agenda or a strategy. I do not know what they are talking about. I have no agenda. I have no strategy. I am not trying to say anything that hasn't already been said a hundred times. I cannot answer the questions you ask me. I do not remember much at all, and I have no reason to remember. Where I have been and where I have come from does not change who I am. I am just the same as everyone else. I came from somewhere, and now I am here…and this is all that matters."

Joseph paused for a moment. He smiled in that inimitable and inscrutable *Joseph* way, and then he said, "We are all looking for a reason…a reason to live, a reason to be, a reason to get out of bed each day and do the best we can. We start out with grand ideas of what we are going to accomplish with our lives, and then we become tired and jaded as the small disappointments and failures mount up. Life, despite the magic we so very much believed in as children, is not magical at all. Expectations are great, accomplishments are few, and we lose sight of what we wanted and what we hoped to achieve. It is all so much harder than we thought. We tell ourselves that our goals were unrealistic and unreasonable. We look for reasons that will explain why we've not become what we intended to be. We forget how to be patient. We forget how to forgive. We harbour resentment and jealousy and petty disagreements. We look at what other people have and we wonder why we don't have it. Krishnamurti said that a life of comparison was a life of misery. We know this to be the truth, and yet we cannot let go of the envy we feel toward others. Bukowski said 'We're all going to die, all of us...what a circus! That alone should make us love each other but it doesn't. We are terrorized and flattened by trivialities. We are eaten up by nothing.'"

Joseph paused to open the bottle of water. He poured a little into the glass and took a sip.

The room was hushed. No one said a word.

"And so it is. We cease being the children we once were. Children do not hate. They are taught to hate. Children do not see divisions of colour or religion or race. They see another child. They do not change their attitude towards you because of your clothes or how much money you have or whether or not you are from a different town or city or country. Children do not possess preconceptions. Perhaps the only difference between adults and children is that children trust until they are given a reason not to do so, whereas adults wait until they are given a reason to trust."

One or two cameras flashed. There was a susurrus of turning pages.

"Kindness," Joseph said. "We began with kindness. We began with everything that kindness contains. Compassion, generosity, patience, tolerance, acceptance, forgiveness, understanding. Kindness is simple. It costs nothing. It requires nothing. The simple fact that you are all here says all that needs to be said. A few random acts of kindness have started a movement. Kindness has engaged our hearts and minds. It has reminded people what it is that they love about people...and, more importantly, it has reminded them what it is that they love about themselves."

Joseph took another sip of water.

"And so, with a few words, a few simple deeds, there are millions of people who have connected to something that anyone can do. You do not need to be rich or smart or powerful or anything else. You do not need to drive a car or have a degree or own your own home or even have a job to be kind. None of us get to the end of our lives and think of all the people we should have been meaner to, only those to whom we should have been *more* kind. We think of those to whom we should have listened, those we should have acknowledged, those we should have accepted, forgiven, helped, encouraged and supported. We think of all the times we did something other than what was right. How may lives have been broken apart because a father could not forgive his daughter for marrying a man the father didn't approve of? And then, on his deathbed, that same father sees how many years and how much love he has wasted. He longs to see his daughter, to tell her he's sorry, that he was wrong, but she will have nothing to do with him and he dies heartbroken. And once he is dead, she will be haunted by guilt because she did not permit him to make amends. How much unhappiness has been caused because someone was not prepared to admit they were wrong or impulsive or judgmental or afraid to tell the truth. People love people. It's the most natural thing in the world. We cannot know who we will love until we love them, and sometimes we surprise ourselves most of all."

There was a murmur of recognition in the room.

"I am no one special," Joseph went on. "I am the same kind of human being as everyone else. I do not have any better answers than you. I just say what I think, but I think about what I am going to say before I say it. We have become afraid of ghosts and shadows, but ghosts and shadows are meaningless. We have forgotten who we really are, and in the absence of any real understanding of ourselves we have accepted a multitude of lies. People are not bad. People are not evil. The dangerous people in our society make up a tiny, tiny minority. It does not take a great deal of imagination to see who they are. They are the ones who keep reminding us that life is bad, that things are bound to go wrong, that there is nothing that can be done about it. People should be judged by what they do, not what other people say about them...and here, I am sorry to say, the newspapers and the media are perhaps the most guilty of all."

Joseph was quiet for a moment. What he'd said was received with a combination of recognition and awkwardness by the press collective.

"But that is no criticism, and I have no right to judge. You have fallen into the same trap as everyone else. You write what you think people want to read. Because it's in the newspapers and on the television people then start to think that this is what they are supposed to be interested in. They are afraid to be different. They want to be liked. They want to be accepted. Being different and contentious is a dangerous business. It takes courage to be yourself, especially when you realise how different you are from everyone else. And so we read the newspapers and we watch the television, and we fill our minds and our lives with the banal and unimportant details of other peoples' lives, and we never really consider that our own lives are just as meaningful as anyone else's. No, you may not be a film star. No, you may not be a famous singer...but the simple truth is that no one in the world is as good at being you as you are. No matter who you are, when you die, all that people will remember of you is whether you brought joy or sadness, whether you elevated others or pushed them down...whether or not you made a difference."

There was a murmur of voices. There were as many who responded with a *Sssshhhh*.

"I read books," Joseph said. "I have read a great many books, and I wish I had the time to read a great many more. For many thousands of years people have been telling the truth. Big truths, small truths, it does not matter. Truth is everywhere. No one man possesses a monopoly. We know there is nothing to fear but fear itself. Life is no mystery. We are born, we die, and in between it should be our purpose to do all we can to make others happy. That, perhaps, is the real secret of being human...the real secret to a joyful life."

More pages turned. More cameras flashed.

"No one should dictate how another person should live their life. The rights of human beings are sacred. The right to think, to speak, to act, to believe, to have faith, to love who we want, to share our lives and experiences and words and emotions with whoever we choose. These are rights that belong to all of us, and no one should be able to take them away. They will try, just as they have tried in the past, but if anything is worth fighting for it is that."

Joseph looked out across the room. It was as if everyone in the room was in thrall of each word he uttered.

"The things I say are other peoples' words," he continued. "The things I say have been said time and again by far wiser people than me. We think that all our time is behind us, but it is not. Our time is ahead and onward into a never-ending future. Yes, it is true, you cannot change yesterday. Yesterday is gone. All the more reason never to give it another thought. You *can* change today, and what you do today will always change the tomorrows that are still to be. We, as a race, possess all the necessary resources and intellect to solve the problems of the world. We can cure illness and disease. We can feed everyone for a fraction of the cost it takes to fight a war. We can solve the problems of famine and drought and climate change and religious intolerance and racial division. Like Jerry Garcia said, if we had any nerve at all, if we had any real balls as a society, or whatever you need, whatever quality you need, real character, we would make an effort to really address the wrongs in this society, righteously."

Joseph leaned forward. He did not raise his voice, but he was closer to the forest of microphones and his voice filled the room.

"Wars happen because someone wants them to happen. Racism and religious intolerance is fostered and promoted to serve hidden agendas and vested interests...and no matter what is said about democracy and libertarianism, we are no more in control of choosing our government than we are choosing the colour of our hair. This is the way of the world, and we can do nothing but take responsibility for allowing it to happen. Once we have accepted that responsibility, then perhaps, just perhaps, we may be able to do something to change it."

The rumble of voices in the gathering grew audible, ever louder. A man rose to his feet and said, "So what are you proposing? You say that the world needs to change...of course the world needs to change.

Hundreds, thousands, millions of people say the world needs to change, but it doesn't change... wars go on, crime continues, people still hurt and kill one another...and all you're doing is giving us aphorisms and quotes that we've all heard before."

"I am proposing nothing," Joseph said.

"If you have no solution, then what gives you the right to stand up there and - - "

"I did not give myself the right. You gave me the right."

A woman stood up on the other side of the room. "Do you know, Mr. Conrad, that this press conference is being streamed live on the internet, and over twenty million people are listening to you right now?"

"I did not know that, no."

"What do you have to say now that you have the attention of so many?"

"Be kind. Be decent. Be courteous. Be generous. Be patient. Be tolerant. Tell the truth. Expect the truth of your fellow man. Stop worrying about what others think of you. Do not be afraid of being yourself."

"Your politics are left wing," a voice said.

"I have no politics," Joseph said. "Politics are for politicians, and I am not a politician."

The questions started thick and fast then, some of them drowned in the hubbub that was escalating within the ballroom.

"Do you intend to stand for local election?"

"Do you think of yourself as some sort of spokesman for the common man?"

"Did you have sex with an American girl in France?"

"Have you appointed yourself as some sort of messiah?"

"Is it true that you can see ghosts?"

"How did you leave and return to the country with no record at Passport Control?"

"Are you working for the opposition government?"

"Do you make it your business to help out prostitutes?"

"Is this a publicity stunt? What are you trying to sell us?"

Joseph answered none of them. He sat silently, every once in a while taking a sip of water, and he watched and listened as the barrage of voices grew ever louder. Finally it was a cacophony over which no single voice could be heard. It was like listening to twenty or thirty radio stations simultaneously. Still Joseph sat implacable and unmoved.

One of the many photographers came forward and tried to take some close-up photographs. Another photographer, attempting to get even closer, pushed him aside. A scuffle broke out. Someone punched someone. A woman started screaming obscenities.

Joseph was waiting for everyone to quieten down, but no one seemed interested in being quiet.

Another disagreement erupted on the far left of the room. The doors at the back were forced open and ten or fifteen people elbowed their way into the press conference.

Security was called, and there was even more shouting and shoving and swearing.

"Mr. Conrad?"

Joseph turned to see Algie Blackwood to his right.

"Best come with me, sir. This is a madhouse."

Joseph took one more look at the ever-growing wave of bedlam and said, "Yes, perhaps that is best."

39

Dadd viewed the section of CCTV footage several times over. There was no doubt in his mind. Joseph Conrad, even now spouting trite banalities and meaningless aphorisms to a pack of idiotic journalists, had been hit by a white van on the very same day as the hospital visit. Conrad had been on a bicycle, and the van had blindly hurtled down a narrow sidestreet and knocked Conrad flying. The bicycle, buckled and twisted, was thrown in the opposite direction, and the van just kept on going. There was no way the driver could not have known, and yet he chose to flee the scene of the accident. Dadd noted the registration plate of the van. Within minutes he had ascertained that the plate belonged to a scrapped Vauxhall.

So, Conrad had indeed been injured, and not lightly. Perhaps no broken bones or dislocated joints, but the impact of his head on the pavement as he came off the bicycle must have been considerable.

Conrad had lain there immobile for more than ten minutes before someone stopped, determined that he was unconscious and called the emergency services.

An ambulance had arrived and Conrad had been delivered to the nearest hospital.

There, as confirmed by the reports from Clara Balfour and the hospital's internal CCTV, Conrad had been examined, left unattended and then just walked out of the building.

No sooner had Dadd finished watching the film than he received another call.

"We have something," he was told. "It's going to your drop box as we speak."

Dadd viewed the new footage. Again, unmistakably, Joseph Conrad, this time a little unsteady on his feet, heading south away from the hospital. He was visible for no more than thirty seconds, but it proved Dadd's assumption that Conrad had just walked out of the hospital and disappeared. Somehow he'd made it home, and thence to work again the subsequent Monday morning. Following his post-accident return, his supervisor, Menella Smedley, had perhaps not been the only one to notice Conrad's change in attitude and demeanour, creating the impression that he was *challenged*, even intentionally irritating. It seemed that Conrad had been suffering some sort of head trauma, evidences of memory loss and disorientation. Now he was being paraded on the television and upheld as some sort of pseudo-messianic sage for the common people. Social media had been responsible for this. Prior to the internet, something such as this could never have happened, or it would have happened so slowly that it could have been controlled and curtailed at will.

Dadd had watched Conrad's performance on-line. It was tantamount to political subversion, an incitement to popular revolt, and it had to be stamped on. Hard.

Dadd's phone rang as soon as Conrad was escorted from the hotel ballroom.

The instructions he was given were clear, concise, impossible to misinterpret.

Dadd ended the call and smiled.

Housework. That's what it was. Just keeping the house in good order. We all had to live in the house together, and upsetting the *status quo* was just not on.

Dadd checked out. He made three calls from the car and arranged a face-to-face meeting with some associates.

256

Within three hours, five at most, this whole circus would have packed up its tents and left town for good.

40.

Algie Blackwood drove Joseph to a different hotel. The streets for a good twenty or thirty yards in each direction were thronged with people. Bars and restaurants were jammed with people, the televisions all playing the same channel. It was like World Cup final night, but it was mid-morning.

"You really are stirring up a hornet's nest," Algie said. "There's going to be a few noses out of joint about all of that. They don't like it when someone upsets the status quo, do they?"

Joseph didn't reply. He felt the pressure in his head. It had been growing for a while, and he knew there was nothing he could do to ease it or stop it.

He smiled. Algie saw that smile in the rearview and smiled back.

"You are a brave man, Mr. Conrad. I'll say that much. You've said some things that people don't want to hear, and yet they know they have to hear them. The bankers, the finance people, the politicians, they're all in this together. They fund the wars and the drug companies and the media, and they all live out of each others' pockets. People aren't stupid. They know this, but what can they do?"

Algie glanced back at Joseph. Joseph wore that faint smile, the one that said everything and nothing.

"Cohesion, that's what it is. Alignment of purpose, you know? That's what social media has given us. People find something and they have a way to share it with other people, thousands of people, millions. That's what's happened here. What you said is right. The things you're saying have been said before, but you had to read books to find them. People don't read books any more, not like they used to, and the education system went down the pan years ago. What do we have now – three, four generations of people who can't and don't read? It's a tragedy. Here, in England, where we publish more books than most places in the world. A wonderful language. Shakespeare, for God's sake!"

Algie shook his heads resignedly.

"It is a tragedy, Mr. Conrad. We have this wonderful language and we don't use it. What happened to us? When did we become so terrified of talking to one another? When did we become so afraid of speaking our minds and being ourselves and telling the truth, eh? We're nothing but big kids, aren't we?"

Algie laughed, but his laughter was brief.

"You don't have kids, I know. I have two. Two boys. Troublemakers, the pair of them. Eight and eleven years old. They lark about, they play games, they wind each other up something terrible. Every once in a while they'll get up to some real mischief, do something really stupid. Like one time they thought it would be a good idea to throw stones over the fence into the neighbour's garden. Crash, smash, half a dozen windows in his greenhouse. I collar the pair of them, they're in floods of tears, they're sorry...hell, at least they're not lying to me, telling me it wasn't them. Anyway, me and the missus calm them down, and we're asking them what happened, why they did this. My eldest, because I know he's the ringleader...I look him in the eye and I say what on earth inspired you to start throwing stones over the neighbour's fence? And you know what he said? Same thing he always says when he's done something really dumb. It seemed like a good idea at the time."

Algie laughed again. "Kids," he said. Gotta love 'em, even when they drive you nuts. Anyway, the point of telling you that, Mr. Conrad, is that we're no different, are we? I mean, even as adults. We do what we think is the right thing. Even when we do those really crazy dumb things, we do them because we figured it was a good idea at the time. Sometimes we hurt the people we love the most by trying to do what we think is right. What do they say? The road to Hell is paved with good intentions."

Algie looked in the rearview. Joseph had closed his eyes.

"Exhausted," Algie said, almost to himself. "Guy must be bloody exhausted. Couldn't bear it myself, all those people running after you shouting at you, asking you questions. Barmy stuff. Absolutely barmy." He took one more look at Joseph as he drew to a halt against the curb. "Hell of a thing," he said. "The amount of trouble you can cause when you try to make a difference."

Algie put his hazards on and got out of the car.

A black cab came up behind him. The driver leaned out of the window and waved.

Algie walked back. "Sorry, mate," he said. "Won't be a moment. Just dropping someone off."

"You've got Joseph Conrad in there, haven't you? I saw you leave the hotel."

"I have yes. I think he's fallen asleep, poor sod. The man must be exhausted."

"You think it'd be alright if I came and shook his hand. Hell of a thing he's doing. Never seen anything like it. Drivers tellin' me every day how polite people are being, people cab-sharing, all sorts of things. Friend of mine told me that he took a fare up from Piccadilly the other day, going out to east Dulwich or someplace. Hammerin' down with rain, it was, and there was this old dear at the bus stop. Fare told my mate to pull over, said he'd give him an extra tenner to pick her up and take her wherever. Gave him the tenner, paid the old dear's fare as well. Amazin'."

"I'm sure he wouldn't mind," Algie said. "Let me go wake him up."

Algie walked back to his car and opened the door.

"Mr. Conrad," he said gently. "Got a man here who wants to shake your hand."

Joseph didn't stir.

"Mr. Conrad," Algie said, and he leaned in to touch Joseph's shoulder.

41.

"A complete discreditation, of course," Dadd said. "No room for extrication. Incontrovertible evidence."

The three men facing him were all ex-military intelligence. Hard eyes, rugged features, shorn hair, creating between them an ominous aura.

"Clean, uncomplicated, that's what we need. Child sex images on a hard drive, membership of some paedophile ring. Something of this nature. I leave it to your judgement and experience, but it needs to be fast."

The man on the left looked up from his smartphone. "I think we're done," he said quietly.

Dadd frowned.

The man handed his phone to Dadd.

A live feed was running from a news website.

CONRAD DEAD the headline announced.

"What the hell?" Dadd asked.

"Seems your boy is done for," the man said. "Dead in the back of a private hire car."

Dadd could not believe his eyes.

The man on the right shook his head. "Surreal. The whole thing has been surreal."

"I saw that press conference thing," the middle man said. "Thought to myself that the worst thing that can happen now is for him to die."

Dadd looked up.

The man smiled knowingly. "The tyrant dies and his rule is over, the martyr dies and his rule begins."

The man on the left looked at his associate.

"Kierkegaard," the man in the middle said. "I read it in a book."

42.

"None of it makes sense," the coroner said. "I see the facts, I look at the evidence, I perform the autopsy, I read the admission notes from the original bicycle accident…and none of it makes sense."

"You're going to have to make a statement," the assistant coroner said.

"I know."

"You have any idea what's going on out there. People are lining the streets. The place has gone mad. It's worse than when Diana died. It's happening in France, Italy, America, Australia…"

"You don't think I'm aware of that?" the coroner asked, his voice tinged with irritation. "I see the newspapers, the stuff on the internet - - "

"Eighty million followers on the Facebook obituary page."

The coroner shook his head. "Yeah, and I'm one of them for Christ's sake."

"So what are you going to say?"

"That he died of a brain haemorrhage. That's the truth."

"Yes, we know he died of a brain haemorrhage, but he didn't die two days ago."

"You don't think I can't see that?"

"It doesn't make sense."

The coroner sighed. He looked at his assistant and raised his eyebrows. "We're now just repeating the same things to one another that we've been repeating for an hour."

"So, what do we know? He had a bicycle accident. According to the admission reports, he suffered a significant head trauma. That created significant haemorrhaging, and yet despite this significant – and by all accounts – fatal haemorrhaging, he somehow managed to get up off the exam table, put his clothes on, leave the hospital, go back to work, get made redundant, travel through France, Ireland and the United Kingdom, start a worldwide movement, give interviews to the press, make television appearances, and then right after giving a press conference that is watched by more people than a royal wedding, he is driven away from the hotel and ten minutes later he's dead."

"Yes," the coroner said. "That's exactly what we know."

"But dead from an injury that was sustained in the bicycle accident."

"That's what the evidence is telling us."

"Okay."

"Okay."

The coroner looked once more at the body on the table. "If we issue that as a statement there will be a riot."

"Yes."

"So what do we say?"

"You're the coroner. You have to sign that, not me."

"You know what we do?"

"What?"

"We do the kindest thing we can do. We do what Joseph would have wanted us to do."

"And what is that?"

"We tell them that he died painlessly and peacefully."

"Of what?"

"A brain aneurysm."

"But that's not true."

"I am the city coroner. If I say it's true, then it's true."

The assistant coroner didn't speak for a moment, and then she shook her head and said. "Yes, okay. I think that's what we should do."

"This conversation never took place."

"What conversation?" she asked. "I haven't the faintest clue what you're talking about."

The coroner smiled. He put his arm around her shoulder. "Best assistant coroner in the world."

"That's very kind of you to say so, sir."

43

The young man facing her reminded Menella Smedley of Martin Freeman. His manner was very pleasant, and after just a few minutes she felt very much at ease in his company.

"I think that's all the formalities," she said. "I don't think there's anything else I need to know."

The young man smiled. His name was Rudyard Kipling.

"I think we're safe to say that the job is yours, Mr. Kipling."

"Rudyard," he said. "Just call me Rudyard."

Menella smiled. "I would tell you that you have an unusual name, but I think I win the competition there."

"You have a very pretty name," he said. "Also very unusual, but very pretty."

"Why, thank you. That is very kind."

"Rudyard is actually my middle name. My first name is Joseph, but I never use it. Some people call me Rudy, but that sounds so American. However, I don't mind."

"We shall call you whatever you wish to be called."

"Thank you."

"You understand that you're filling a position that has been vacated," Menella said.

"Yes, I do."

"And you know who used to do this job before you?"

Rudyard Kipling smiled so warmly, so effortlessly and everything in the world seemed so very simple.

"Everything will be fine," Rudyard said. "I can pick up just where he left off."

"It was so sad," Menella said. "What happened was so very sad."

"He was a free soul," Rudyard said. "A free soul is rare, but you know it when you see it, basically because you feel good, very good, when you are near or with them."

Menella smiled. "That is a beautiful thing to say."

"Bukowski said that," Rudyard replied. "Charles Bukowski. He also said that you have to die a few times before you can really live."

"Yes," Menella said. "Yes, indeed."

"I shall see you on Monday, then."

"Yes, of course," she replied. "I'm looking forward to working with you, Mr. Kipling."

Kipling smiled that charming and artless smile once more, and then he closed the door silently behind him.

Menella sat for a little while with a strange sense of inner calm, and she knew that everything was going to be alright.

Printed in Great Britain
by Amazon